REVELATION

*The divine or supernatural disclosure
to humans of something relating to
human existence or the world*

Kaye Harrison

Harrison Harbor, LLC

Paperback ISBN: 979-8777880727

First Paperback edition December 2021
Edited by Deborah Holder
Cover art by Fiona Jayde Media

DEDICATION

This book is dedicated to my husband, children and my mom. Without all your support this story would not exist.

ACKNOWLEDGMENTS

I would like to take the opportunity to thank all those who have helped me with the creation of this book. Your generosity of time and support was a gift I hope to one day repay.

To my husband Jim, I want to tell you how much I appreciate you recognizing my dream and supporting me through it. Many late nights and long days you had to be without me. Thank you for understanding, I love you forever.

I want to thank my sons Tristan and Brandon who had to read and re-read parts of my story. Thank you for your input, I truly appreciate your desire to see me succeed. You made me laugh and helped me keep the creep factor in the story. It was a joy to include you on my journey. I love you both very much.

To my mother, Jane. I cannot thank you enough for your encouragement to follow this dream. I appreciate you being my first "line-of-defense" in editing and creation. Sorry you had to read, re-read and re-read again this story so many times. But your input was so valuable to me, and I can't thank you enough. Thanks for pushing me to reach my goals, I love you.

A big thank you goes to my best friend and Editor, Debby Holder. All the nights we worked on re-writes were hard, crazy and full of laughter. I will value every moment we shared together. Thank you for believing in me and encouraging me to finish what I started. All those times I didn't believe in myself, you helped me see what I couldn't. I love you, my friend.

To the McIntyre's, you lead by example. Thank you for your generosity of time and teaching me. I could have never done any of this without your input and for letting me pick your brains! I appreciate you and hope I can one day repay your kindness.

My friend Heather Rinn, thank you for helping me get started. Your input was invaluable. I also want to thank you for the time you spent gathering and sending me information. It was definitely a learning process! Your help and support were appreciated.

To my best friend Diane Simpson, thank you for the pep talks and the reassurances that this dream was possible. You helped me see the possibilities of a dream that could come true. Thank you so much, I love you, my friend.

This has been a passion project for me, and I hope everyone that reads this book enjoys the story as much as I had creating it. I cannot thank you enough to all who will read this book, your time is priceless to me. Book number two shouldn't be too far away, so stay in touch and God bless you all.

Revelation

Kaye Harrison

.

Prologue

Standing under the old oak tree Jaxon looked at the scene in front of him. So many memories, so much love, so much sorrow. It hurt his heart as he turned his head to look at his childhood home. He missed his mom and his sister, hell, he almost had a longing to hear his stepfather's demands. That relationship had been turbulent, and he didn't know what to believe about that man anymore.

Charles was easy to anger and had treated him unfairly. Jaxon knew it. There was suspicion surrounding the accident. Charles had been there when it happened. He had seen his stepfather running out of the barn and kneeling over the body after the fall.

Charles had roared for Jaxon's mother to come to him. Hearing the alarm in his voice, she ran out of the house and saw where the body lay. She began screaming and wailing hysterically throwing herself over her son's lifeless body. Jaxon watched as his stepfather jumped up and pulled his mom up into his arms, holding her, trying to bring her back from her anguish and heartbreak. She was beyond wild with grief - shrieking, kicking, and clawing at him to release her. She needed to break free and return to the body that lay there.

Jaxon's heart sank, wondering what was going to happen to them, his mother and his sister. They would have to work through their grief. He looked back at the little fenced in area where he stood in the shade from the tree as the sun's rays filtered through the leaves. It was a beautiful sight, but all he could feel was sorrow as he read the headstone in the family cemetery, *Jaxon Harrison Hanley.*

Chapter 1

"Seriously?!!" I exclaimed.

"Alisa Renee Christi! Its only for six months, don't be so dramatic," my mother scolded.

"But what about my summer plans, my job and my Senior year of high school? What about all my friends?" I felt the desperation setting in. My mom had just told me she was leaving for six months to work in another country. What was worse, she had already made plans for me to stay with my aunt and uncle while she was gone. I was furious! She didn't even *think* about discussing this with me before she went ahead and said yes to her job. She was making plans about my life without my input. I was old enough to make decisions for myself. To think for myself! It would have been nice if she had taken the time to consider my opinion regarding this issue.

Mom sighed, trying to keep her patience. "You know what a big opportunity this is for me to work in England, Alisa. Besides, I have already made all the arrangements for us. We're going to pack up the house and rent it for six months, while you will stay with your aunt and uncle." She laid her hand on my arm. It was her way to give me consolation about the move. Looking me in the eyes and trying to sound upbeat she continued. "And when I return from England, we can come back! You will be able to graduate with the rest of your class. As for work, I'm sure you can find something to do at your aunts to earn money and your friends can call you anytime they want!"

She made it sound so easy, like out of sight never meant out of mind. My friends would go on with their lives and forget all about me. I just knew it. Didn't she remember what it was like to be a teenager? We don't just talk on the phone. We like to get together and go to a movie, go shopping, or simply hang out. I knew I was being a little melodramatic, but what the hell? I was upset! I can be dramatic if I want to. Isn't that a requirement of being a teenager? To be dramatic? However, I knew it would be a lost cause to argue with my mother. "What's done is done," I mumbled in despair. There was no way of changing my mother's mind when she had made a final decision.

My mom was a scientist and worked hard in the field of medical research. I knew she deserved this opportunity to do what she loved overseas. I always tease her about *being a brainiac, trying to save the world!* I looked at my mother again and sighed; she was a force to be reckoned with. I have always considered my mom, Jennifer Christi, a superpower. She stood about five feet six inches and was full of energy. I saw my mom as an attractive and stylishly put together woman. In fact, if I were being honest, I felt a little inferior to her, not that it was a competition. But I was bland to her spit-and-polished look.

Mom's hair is sandy blonde, and she has green eyes like mine, but that is where the similarities end. I am slightly shorter and have more curves than her. Mom tells me all the time that it's a blessing to be curvy. However, I don't feel quite the same. It makes me feel heavy and awkward, especially when I am running. Now *that* is my passion. There is nothing more fulfilling to me than running. It provides me with a feeling of freedom, and it helps clear my mind.

If there was one feature about me that I would never change, it was my hair. My hair color is the same as moms, but unlike hers, mine has always been thick and wavy. It's long and falls to the middle of my back. I usually wear it in a ponytail because it's easier to manage, plus I need it off my neck when I run. It makes me chuckle when mom says she is jealous of my hair. I'm glad to have at least one thing better than her.

When I'm not wearing my hair in a ponytail, I leave it down. I just run my fingers through it, and it stays wherever it falls. When comparing my fashion to my mom's, let's just say I am definitely not my mother! Most days, I am in my running gear head to toe, with my famous ponytail bobbing around. While mom is professionally dressed in her suits and blouses.

Thinking about my passion for running, I needed to leave right now. I had to get outside and go for a jog. I didn't want to cry and act like a child in front of my mother, so jogging was the best option. It would clear the cloud of emotions building inside of me. I had to digest mom's pronouncement of my forced move. I slid my shoes on and started for the door.

"Alisa, please … don't leave right now," my mom called out to me. "Don't you think we should talk about this?"

"I have to go," I said holding back my tears. "I need to process … all of this," I said as I wildly waved my hand around in the air. "We'll talk about it when I get back," I said, slamming the door as I went out. The sound matched my mood.

I started running and felt the tears escaping the corners of my eyes. I wiped them away and kept running, waiting for all my feelings to melt from within. I needed to make sense of this new life I was about to embark on. New school, new friends (hopefully) and what about all my friends I am leaving here? As an only child, my friends were everything to me. I spent a lot of time with them since mom worked so much. My best friend, Nikki, was like family to me. We pretty much lived in each other's homes. Hopefully, it would just be gone and not forgotten with my friends. Saying goodbye would be so hard to do.

Later that day I decided to call my best friend Nikki and tell her that I was leaving. Nikki Carino and I had been best friends since second grade. We had been waiting excitedly for our senior year thinking about prom and graduation. "I can't believe it!" I exclaimed. "Mom just springs it on me that we have to move because she's leaving the country to work in England. And to make matters worse, I have to go live with my aunt and uncle in Cedar Mills, Maryland. That's four hours away from here! What am I going to do without you? "

"Oh Alisa, how long are you going to be gone for?" Nikki asked, her voice wavering.

"Six months."

"Six months! Are you freaking kidding me?! What the hell, Alisa! How am I going to survive without you for that long?" I heard the sniffling coming from the other end of the phone. "This was our big year!"

Please don't cry, don't cry, don't cry or I'll fall apart too I thought to myself. Our emotions were high, considering that my mom's decision rocked our whole world. I depended on Nikki. I spend just as much time with her family as I do my own. Mom doesn't have a whole lot of time due to her work, taking care of a house, paying bills, and oh yeah, me! I understand it. She carries a lot on her shoulders since she was by herself with no partner to share the responsibilities. But while she was focusing on her career it had slowly become her life. She spent a lot of time in the lab, bringing papers home to research and reports to write. Her focus did not leave much room for anyone or anything else. Including me ... at least, that is how it felt sometimes.

Hearing the devastation in Nikki's voice I knew that it was hitting her hard and I could feel her sadness. Nikki was a true friend. She had never left my side longer than a day or two. Except for that time her family decided to go to Florida, and she called me from every ride she went on at Disney World.

"Don't cry Nikki, we can figure something out. Maybe you can come visit me in '*The Country*,'" I twanged out. "*And you can call me all the time!*" I said trying to sound cheerfully southern, but I knew it was a load of crap.

"Maybe," she sniffed up a tear. I could almost hear her smile on the other end of the phone as she heard me making fun of my new existence. I just knew going to the country in Cedar Mills, where the most exciting thing is riding a tractor, would totally suck. I was a suburban girl. I liked my neighborhoods, shopping malls and all the conveniences of our populous town. The country was nothing but grass, dirt and trees with a house speckled in here and there. *Don't even think about it right now*, I told myself, plenty of time to sulk later.

"Will you please come over and help me pack?" I asked. "I'll let you pick out some things to hold on to until I get back." I said, sweetening the deal.

"Really?" There it was. The sound of her voice brightened, and I knew I had hooked her. "Then count me in! Nothing like shopping at the Christi's," she laughed, "besides, I need some new shirts, maybe a pair of jeans."

She sounded awful cheerful, I thought chuckling to myself. "Hey! Jeans are off limits. Going to need those when I'm milking a cow or sowing a field," I laughed. She knew it wasn't true. I have never worked on my aunt and uncle's farm; I only went for visits. I finally had her laughing which made us feel better and knowing I would be seeing her shortly made it even more tolerable.

Can I say packing a room sucks! In fact, packing a whole house sucks even more! But I had my bestie at my side working along with me. Nikki and I had gone through every square inch of my room, and she had a box full of things to show for it. I didn't mind giving her the stuff, after all, it is only stuff. What do I need with it? She is my best friend and I wanted her to have it. Something to keep her thinking of me.

I smiled to myself and turned to Nikki. "Let's get back to work, 'cause I know you're going to want more."

"You know it! Best friend sharesies, right?!"

Laughing I reached over and pulled her in to me, "Best friends forever" I said giving her a big hug.

Chapter 2

I could see the excitement of Aunt Valerie's face when we pulled up. She waved and raced over to the car with that big smile she loves to give. "Jennifer! Alisa! Finally, you made it!" she said with excitement in her voice. "I hope the trip here wasn't too terrible," she said eying her sister. Aunt Valerie knew how my mom hated driving. But I loved it! That's why I always drove when we went on a trip.

"It wasn't bad at all since I had Alisa do the driving. Of course, I had to remove my death grip from the dashboard a couple of times," she said, raising her eyebrows at me. I just rolled my eyes. "Nothing like a road trip to bring people together!" Mom laughed as she pulled Valerie in for a giant hug.

Aunt Valerie turned to me and pulled me into her arms, giving me one of her infamous giant hugs. "And you my dear, are as gorgeous as ever!" she exclaimed. Aunt Valerie Naylor was my favorite adult. More like a mentor and confident, but I'd never tell mom. I can talk to her about anything, and she is always there to give me the right answers. Seeing them side by side, I can see the similarities to my mom. She had the same coloring, same green eyes that dominate our family gene pool, same hair as my mother except it's more of a strawberry blonde than sandy. Personally, I think that color comes from a bottle, but I would never say it aloud.

"Well, there you all are, so glad you are finally here," Uncle Henry said, throwing his hat on his head as he walked over to the car to help with my luggage. "Thought I was going to have to bolt Valerie's feet to the floor since she was so excited about you two coming. Especially you," he said as he tapped my nose. "Get in here!" he said as he picked me up and swung me around in his arms.

Good, sweet Uncle Henry Naylor, or Uncle H as I like to call him. Our family farmer! I would have never pinned my aunt as a farmer's wife, but she seems so happy here. Uncle Henry has made a great life for them as a farmer. He planted acres and acres of soybean crops to sell. He also plants a vegetable garden for Aunt Valerie every year. She says he does it to keep her busy and out of his hair, but secretly I know he does it because she loves it.

Looking at him, I could see the draw for my aunt. He is rather nice to look at with his strong features and constant stubble. His skin is tanned by the sun from working outside and is set off by his dark curly hair speckled with a little gray. He claims Aunt Valerie gave him the gray from all her antics! I always laugh when he says this because it is probably true. But he loves her, zany behavior, and all. I have caught him in those special moments when he looks at her. Total adoration. I love how that one look can make my aunt blush, especially when people are around to see it. Uncle H balances Aunt Val with a calm about him, as if he is always in control of every situation and nothing riles him. He is the perfect fit for the crazy in this family.

I inhaled deeply and was thrown back to the summers when I was a kid, running all over this farm.

The smell of summer heat mixed with raw earth and my aunts freesias blooming in the yard was an instant reminder of what I had missed. My memories of this place are some of the happiest times of my childhood.

I looked over at the house and noticed nothing had changed. The house was your typical two-story farmhouse, with white siding and black shutters complete with a cozy front porch outfitted with a swing and a couple of rockers. But it was the enclosed side porch we used to come in and out of the house. With windows all around that opened to provide a much-needed breeze on a hot summer day or that closed to offer a front row seat to watch the summer storms roll by. It has always been our favorite place to gather, whether spending time together or entertaining when company stops by.

Uncle Henry took my luggage upstairs to the room at the end of the hall next to the bathroom. This had always been "my room" ever since I can remember. I never understood why they needed a four-bedroom house - my aunt and uncle were never blessed with any children. I didn't know if that was by their will or God's. I had always been curious, but too afraid to ask since it's really none of my business.

After unpacking and getting settled in, I met up with my mom, aunt and uncle in the kitchen. Aunt Valerie was putting the final touches on what looked to be an amazing dinner. The smells of pot roast filled the air. Mom and I looked at each other and grinned knowing that a feast was about to begin! My mom nodded her head to the side and glanced towards the living room. I knew she wanted to talk to me alone, so I followed her and sat down on the couch.

"You best be careful while living here; your aunt would love nothing better than to stuff you like a potbelly pig," my mom teased.

"Not to worry. I will keep up my running routine. Lots of flat land here to go the distance. Plus, I plan on helping around the farm, keeping busy until school starts." I paused and fidgeted for a moment. "Speaking of school, I'm so nervous about going to a new one. I hate the idea of starting over and trying to make friends temporarily until I go home. What if they don't want a newcomer just sticking around for a few months? It is their senior year, after all, and these kids have all grown up together in this small town."

Mom looked at me thoughtfully; she knew this was not an ideal situation for me to go through as a senior in high school. She got up out of the chair she was sitting in and came over to sit beside me on the couch. Leaning towards me she enveloped me into a big hug. Stroking my hair and back, she held me for a few moments.

"You, my love, are going to be fine. You're so amazing that those kids would be fools not to want to be your friend. You're smart, beautiful and have a kind heart. I'm the one that is sad to be missing a part of your last year in high school. Can you forgive me? I'm so sorry for taking you away from your life at home." I could see the guilt written all over her face. I didn't want mom to leave feeling that way. So, I bucked up and gave her a big smile. "Please don't feel bad mom; there is nothing to forgive. I really am excited that you get to go to Europe. I just hope you will get to see more than the insides of a laboratory."

My mom laughed at that, knowing it was completely possible to spend all her time in the lab. When she was focused on her research, the rest of the world didn't exist. "I just want you to be happy, my love, that's what matters most to me," she said as she gave my hand a squeeze.

"You know I will be fine. Aunt Val is going to make sure of that. Plus, you and I can call, skype or email each other all the time. That way I can keep you up to date on all the happenings here. Besides, if anyone should worry about someone, it'll be me worrying about you. Who is going to take care of you while you are away? You know how you misplace your things sometimes!" I gave her a quick hug back as we both chuckled. Again, she knew I was right.

"Listen, I've already registered you for school and Aunt Val is going to take you shopping for your summer reading books. If you need some clothes, shoes, or anything, I have a credit card I am giving you to use for these things. Please be responsible with it and only use it for necessities." She got up and retrieved the card from her purse and handed it to me.

"Thanks Mom, I'm going to run this up to my room." I paused for a moment, and I could tell she was feeling down. Looking at her, I added "I love you, Mom; I'll be okay." I smiled at her, and she gave me the *I hope so* smile back. I ran the rest of the way upstairs to my room and was putting the card in my wallet when I heard my aunt sing out, "Dinner's ready!".

Staying up late into the night, my mom and I talked and laughed with my aunt about the capers she always seemed to get into around town and with poor

Uncle Henry. A while later, I left them to finish catching up, since they would not be seeing each other for a while. Plus, I knew they wanted to talk about me. Mom was probably filling Aunt Val in on the conversation we had earlier; I was sure of it.

The next morning came too quickly and it was getting close to the time my mom would have to leave. I could already feel the ache in my chest that I would not be seeing her for a long while. We finished our breakfast and Uncle H took her small bag of luggage to the car.

"I wish you could stay for a few days longer," I told my mother, feeling the tears burning behind my eyes. I didn't want to let her go just yet; six months suddenly felt like an eternity to me. I would miss our late-night talks and our occasional movie nights. I would miss our shopping trips, and going out to dinner together, because who wants to cook? Technology is just not the same as having her here.

"I have to go today. I kept you with me longer than I probably should have and now I have so much more to do before I leave for England. It seems like every time I think I'm ready, I learn that something else has to be done!" Mom grabbed onto my arms and held them firm. Looking into my eyes, she spoke from her heart. "I love you sweetheart. I really do hate leaving you."

"I know Mom, we talked about this. I understand it's only temporary."

"I want you to keep in touch with me as often as you can." she requested, tracing my face with her fingers. It was almost as if she was trying to claim every detail of it to memory. "We will be together again in no time. I promise. And don't give your aunt and uncle any problems." Giving me one final hug and a kiss on my cheek, she turned to her sister Valerie. "Thank you from the bottom of my heart for doing this. I don't know what I would have done without you and Henry taking care of my girl."

"The pleasure is ours," Valerie replied. "You know we love her as if she were our own. Now is my chance to try on motherhood to a teenager fulltime."

"Great, here comes more gray hairs," Uncle Henry said sarcastically with a grin.

"Hey, you know you love me!" I shouted and hit my uncle playfully on the arm

With one last look at the three of us, mom got in her car and drove off waving for as long as I could see her. When she was finally out of sight, the tears came, and the sobs rang out. I had played the brave card throughout this entire move, but now it was done, and I felt all the pent-up emotions hit me at once. Aunt Valerie rushed over and pulled me into her arms to comfort me. Nothing needed to be said as she let me cry it out.

Chapter 3

After a few days of settling in and spending quality time with my aunt and uncle, I was getting restless looking for something to do that would not make me feel in the way. I didn't want to ever be a burden to my aunt and uncle since they had graciously brought me into their home full time. As I walked down the stairs, Aunt Valerie called out to me. "Alisa, would you come here for a minute?"

"I'm right here, looking for you!" I surprised my aunt with my presence. Valerie's head snapped up in surprise and we both laughed.

"I was just finishing this cake and have a few jars of pickled beets over there that I would like for you to take across the road to the neighbors, if you would please." She asked.

Shaking my head yes, as I spoke. "Absolutely! I was looking for something to do anyway."

"Oh dear, you're not getting bored with us already, are you?" Aunt Val asked, with a pensive look on her face.

"No, that is not it at all!" I exclaimed. "On the contrary, I don't want to bug the two of you all the time and get in your way."

"Sweetheart, you could never bug us or get in our way. I don't want you feeling that way, ever! Just having you here brightens our days," she said as she reached over and grabbed my chin and shook it gently. I felt the love my aunt was throwing my way and I smiled back. "That's better," she said, "I love to see that beautiful smile of yours."

Watching my aunt pack everything into a basket for the neighbors. I was excited about going across the road to their house. I had been coming here to visit all my life and over the years I had met some of the neighbors around here. I had even gone visiting with my aunt and uncle to some of their farms. Never had I, however, been to the house across the road. I've always wanted to. It was a founding house in Cedar Mills which meant it was historic. I loved the idea of so much history in a house with its original features - large columns on the front porch and the old brick exterior.

The old farmhouse was beautiful but always felt off limits, like it commanded respect and permission to enter. The truth is, I never went over there because it had been empty when I was young. I had been afraid to roam around the property. I would worry that I was somehow doing something wrong. So, I never took the chance.

"Okay, I'm all finished, are you ready to go?" Aunt Valerie asked.

"Absolutely!" I said grabbing for the basket.

"Alisa, put the basket down just for a moment. I need to let you know something about our neighbors."

Frowning, I put the basket back down on the table. "What are you going to tell me? They aren't like bad people or something? I'm not going to be attacked, am I?" I shivered at the thought.

Aunt Val chuckled out loud, "Oh, no, no, no, my dear, nothing as terrible as that! I just wanted to give you a heads up that our neighbors have been going through a real tough time. About a year ago, they lost their oldest child, and it has been especially hard for the mother, Grace."

"Oh my gosh, what happened?!"

"It was an accident; her son was pulling haybales up into the upper portion of the barn. As he was pulling on the rigging for the hay, somehow, he slipped and fell from the forty-foot opening of the barn. It was terribly sad; he was such a nice young man."

"That's horrible! "I can't imagine how awful it would be to lose a child."

"I couldn't either. I usually go over at least once a week to talk to her and try and be of some comfort to Grace. She and I have become close friends over the years, and well, the loss has taken a huge toll on the family. But I really can't go today; your Uncle Henry needs my help on a project he is working on."

I thought for a moment, unsure if Grace would want my company. "I hope she won't mind me coming over instead of you."

"I'm sure she would love to meet you."

I grinned at my aunt, "Good, because I would love nothing more than to get inside that house! I've always wanted to know what it looks like inside. I am sure there are some historic features in there."

"Slow down there, girlie. You need to get to the front porch first!" Aunt Valerie was giving me the 'watch yourself' stare. "You know how they say curiosity killed the cat?"

"Not to worry, I'll behave," I said with one last promising grin. I reached out and grabbed the basket and proceeded to walk over to the neighbor's house.

A main road called Ash Fort Road separated our two properties and the neighbor's house sat at the end of a long dirt driveway. Crossing the road and walking down towards the house, I took in all the sights along the way. Rows and rows of soybean crops flanked each side of the long driveway and kept going around the house towards the back of the property. Who knew how many acres they had? The regal house sat in the middle of all the acreage with a barn off to the left. Which made me wonder if they had any animals.

I looked at the front porch and noticed how beautifully set up it was. There were four rocking chairs across the porch with little tables placed between them. Two large ferns framed the front door and baskets of colorful flowers were placed all around the edge of the porch. Beautiful flowers and shrubs were planted around the front porch, adding color to the front of the yard. A large tree with a tire swing hanging off a branch offered some shade in the front yard on the left. When looking to the right, I noticed a huge old oak tree. It must have been there since the house had been built. *How small it must have been back then, if the house was well over a hundred years old!*

It was there under the old oak tree that a small fenced off area caught my eye. I wandered over briefly to see what was there. It was an old family cemetery. It was so interesting to read all the old headstones of family members that must have lived here at one time or another. Then my eyes fell to the newest headstone in the cemetery. Jaxon Harrison

Hanley, I read his birth date and his death date. He was only eighteen when he died! That was only one year older than me! I could not imagine my life ending at this young of an age. So sad. This cemetery had suddenly become depressing to me, so I turned and walked back towards the house.

This antiquated house and all its history; I was fascinated by it. I was sure there must have been many fun-filled memories here before the tragedy. I let my mind wander and could imagine the house when it was first built in the 1800's. I could easily picture women sitting on the front porch in their long dresses, sipping their lemonade, gossiping over the news of the day.

Suddenly, the front screen door slammed open. Catching my attention, a man marched out of the house with anger in his eyes staring me down. "Who are you and what do you want? If you're trying to sell something, go on and leave. We're not buying a damn thing!"

I stood there taken aback, Aunt Valerie never said anything about this infuriated looking man standing before me. "I'm, uh ... here ... to um see Grace? My Aunt sent me over. We live across the road." I pointed to the house behind me.

Still glaring at me, he yelled, "Grace! Somebody here to see you!" and with a look of irritation still in his eyes he firmly stated, "Don't be hanging around here too long; we have work to do." And with that he marched off towards the barn.

Grace Hanley walked out the front door to greet me. As indignant as her husband was, Grace was the total opposite. She carried herself with a sense of charity and kindness. She held her hand out to welcome me and introduced herself. "My name is Grace as you may have guessed by now, and you are?"

"Alisa, Alisa Christi. I am Valerie's niece from across the road." I responded in kind.

"Oh yes! Valerie told me you were coming to stay with her. She was so excited. I was hoping she was coming over this week to visit me," she said, craning her neck to see if Valerie was walking down the lane behind me.

"Aunt Valerie wasn't able to come today. She is helping my uncle with a project, but she sent me here with a few goodies to give you!" I said, showing her the delectables in my basket.

"That Valerie is too kind. It seems like she is always trying to feed and fatten us up!" She laughed.

"That's Aunt Valerie. Her way of saving the world is feeding it!" I smiled at Grace, taking her in. She was very pretty with her blue eyes and light brown hair. Her hair must have some length to it. She had it pulled up with a clip and some of it was begging to fall out. The whisps of hair that had gotten loose gave a softness to her face. Grace had a small build with delicate features, but I could see the sadness and loss behind those eyes that were trying so hard to be happy.

"Where are my manners? Please come up to the porch. Would you like something to drink? I can get something for you while I take these into the house," she said, taking the basket from my hands.

"No ma'am, I'm fine. I'll wait there, if that is okay?" pointing to one of the rocking chairs on the porch.

I waited for Grace's nod of approval before walking up the porch and sitting down. Grace set the basket into the crook of her arm and went into the house. When she came back, she held two glasses of ice water in her hands and a young girl of about five or six was following her.

"Just in case you get thirsty," she smiled as she handed one of the glasses to me. *Ever the gracious host* I thought.

"Momma, who is this?" The little girl asked.

"Elsie, this is Ms. Valerie's niece Alisa. Alisa, this is my daughter Elsie."

Wow, Elsie was a beautiful child. She looked a lot like Grace with the delicate features and long light brown hair. Her eyes were different from Grace's though, hazel in color and were framed by long thick lashes. *This one's trouble,* I thought; *get you wrapped around her finger in an instant!* With that sweet looking smile and eyes that shone bright, Elsie smiled at me with a toothless grin. "I like your aunt; she's super nice to me. And I really like her cake!" I had to laugh at Elsie because I liked my aunt's cake too.

"Now that you have had your curiosity cured, go on and play," Grace said as she smiled down at her daughter.

"Yes Momma," Elsie sang out as she ran off to play while Grace sat down to talk with me.

"Your Aunt said you were staying for a while."

"Six months, according to my mom's plans," I said wryly. "Sorry, I don't mean to be sarcastic. Just trying to adjust to my new life."

"I totally understand, you're a teenager. Change is hard. I guess you will be going to school here as well. Or have you already graduated?"

"I will be going to school here. I'm a senior, my last year of high school. I'm hoping to get back home before I graduate." I noticed a quick pained look on Grace's face as I spoke, but she quickly replaced it with a smile and went on to ask more questions.

Grace and I spent about an hour together getting to know one another. I really liked her and could see why Aunt Valerie was friends with her. Grace looked off to the barn and thanked me for the visit, stating she had some chores she really needed to get back to. She looked anxious and I got the hint.

I paused struck by a thought. So, I asked, "Hey Grace, if you ever need any help around here, just let me know. I would be happy to help you out!" I knew if anyone needed help, it was this woman, but I had doubt that she would ever ask.

"I might take you up on that. Come back anytime and please, don't let my husband scare you off! Just like your aunt, you are always welcome." Grace turned to go into the house and stopped. She stood there for a long pause then turned back to say, "You know, I could use a visit tomorrow. Can you be here at 1:00 p.m.?"

"Sure! I'll be here." We said our goodbyes and I left just as Grace's husband was coming around to the front of the house. *I am so glad I left before he got back, he gives me the creeps!* I thought to myself.

Later that day I found myself alone with my aunt, and I wanted to talk about our neighbors across the road. I didn't want to gossip, but I couldn't help my curiosity.

I started with, "I hate to say it, but when I first got to their house, the husband acted like an ass! Excuse my language. He started his attack before I was barely able to get the words out to say who I was or why I was there."

"Just because you do not like the way someone talks to you, does not mean they are a bad person. I have spoken to Charles many times and he has always been polite to me. A little intense maybe, but nice. He probably acted that way because he didn't know who you were. Probably thought you were there trying to sell something." She laughed

"I know, Aunt Val. I just like Grace so much. She is so nice, and he seems so mean! Besides, I think she liked me," I mused.

"Oh, and why is that?" She asked as she titled her head, raising her eyebrows at me.

"She asked me to come back tomorrow."

"Well, that is something. That means you must have been on your best behavior; wait till she really gets to know you!" Aunt Val burst out in laughter as I stood there with my mouth wide open – in a display of fake shock.

With my hand on my heart, I said "Aunt Val! How dare you, you know I am a saint." And we both broke out in fits of laughter.

Later that night Nikki and I had one of our daily chats. It was nice that we kept in constant contact. She was really missing me, and I wanted to see her so badly. We chatted about our friends and her job. I mentioned my visit with Grace to her and told her about "the husband". She seemed a little worried about him.

"I hope you are careful when you go over there again. Just try and stay clear of him." Nikki advised.

"What do you think he is going to do to me, Nikki? I'm sure he's not an axe murderer or anything like that!" I laughed.

"Not funny!! Just be careful," she said. After a time, we said our goodbyes and hung up. I went to bed later that night with the Hanley family on my mind, wondering what they had been going through and why Grace said she would 'handle' Mr. Hanley. Was he dangerous? My Aunt did not seem to think so.

As I returned to the Hanley farm the next day, I saw Grace sitting on her front porch in what she would call a rare time to be alone. Alone … she mentioned that word in passing yesterday. It was odd to think of her feeling so alone. She had a husband and a daughter to take care of, but it's understandable how she could feel empty from the death of her son. I've heard losing a child was painful and unbearable. The grief could be immense and the heartbreak overwhelming. Maybe I would be able to offer some comfort to her.

Grace had mentioned yesterday how she missed having a teenager around and was happy that I had come to visit. I think that is why she asked me back today. I noticed Charles' truck was missing and wondered if that is why she made plans for this time of day, knowing we wouldn't have any interruptions.

As I walked closer to the porch, I noticed Grace was holding a dishtowel in her hand. She must have been crying. She heard me approaching and quickly wiped her face off. I'm sure she was hoping I wouldn't notice. Too late.

"Hi Grace, are you okay?" I gently asked.

She looked up at me and tried to act casual. Forcing a smile she responded, "I'm okay. I was just having a moment of weakness."

"I'm so sorry; is there anything I can do to help?" I asked hoping she could see the compassion in my eyes.

I must have inspired her to reveal the emotion she had been holding. Grace paused and took a deep breath letting it out slowly, preparing to bare her feelings. Looking at me she said in a low voice. "I'm not sure your aunt told you, but I lost my oldest child last year. Sometimes when I give myself too much time sitting still, the memories creep in and my grief overtakes me."

My thoughts instantly flashed back to the newest headstone in the family cemetery under the old oak tree. I could sense Grace's overwhelming pain she carried as I continued to listen to her.

"The pain still feels so fresh, Alisa, I'm sorry I can't help crying," she said as she wiped the tears again from her eyes. Taking in another full breath and holding it, almost as if she was willing away the sorrow. "I'm alright now, let's talk about something else."

I knew she was not alright now. I sat down and reached over to touch her arm. "Grace, it's okay. It is good to cry, believe me. I've had many tears myself here lately. Aunt Valerie says it's a washing of the psyche."

Grace finally was able to give me a genuine smile this time. "Your aunt is a treasure!" she remarked. "She is always trying to make me laugh or fatten me up."

"So true!" I laughed. "She does seem to know what to say or what to stuff in my face, depending on the situation." I finally felt like I had broken Grace's sadness and felt her burden of grief slowly lift from her for a moment.

As the laughter died off, I could tell Grace was taking a second to organize her thoughts before she spoke again. She must have decided to open up to me saying, "When I lost my son it shattered me, and I can't even keep a straight thought at times. I never stop working because when I have idle time, I start to think of him. The pain rips through me and it is just too much to bear." I watched as Grace closed her eyes in this honest admission and saw the tears escaping the corners of her eyes.

"Oh Grace, I'm so sorry. Would it be too hard for you to tell me about him?" I asked softly.

Grace braced herself, I could see it. "You know what? I think I'd like to, Alisa. Everyone around here, including your aunt and uncle, had known him for years. So, really I haven't been able to talk about him or describe him in a long while." The thought of her son brought a bittersweet smile to her lips. "His name was Jaxon. Jaxon Harrison Hanley. He was around your age actually. How old are you? Seventeen? Eighteen?"

"Seventeen," I replied.

"I knew it!" she smiled sincerely. Then Grace took a moment of pause and prepared herself to continue her story. "Jaxon was eighteen when we lost him. It was during the summer after graduation from high school and he had so many big plans ahead of him. He was planning on going to college in the fall." She said shaking her head in thought. "He always said he was going to leave this god-forsaken farm, get rich and come take Elsie and me away from here." She laughed bitterly at that statement. I could tell this was a hurtful spot for her, but she went on. "He had been so determined to make a better life for me and his sister. I had to constantly remind him that it was not his job to make us a better life. I wanted, no, needed him to only worry about himself and make a life for himself. Whether or not it would be 'better'," she air-quoted, "was on him."

I smiled at that statement. She sounded just like my mother telling me that I had to make my own destination in life. My outcome in life would be a result of what I made it and that she could not live my life for me. I quickly brought myself back to Grace and her story of Jaxon. Wanting her to continue, I said, "He loved his family Grace, that is a beautiful thing. What else?"

"Thank you for saying that, Alisa." she smiled in agreement. Restarting her description of her son she spoke, "Jaxon was very loving, kind, smart and had a great sense of humor. He was a hard worker without much complaint. Although, he had every right to. Charles was so hard on him at times, that I worried Jaxon had built up a resentment towards him. I would try to talk to Charles about it, but we would end up disagreeing on that issue.

"Jaxon was crazy for animals, especially his horse Grey. And that dang horse loved Jaxon so much, that he gave everyone else an attitude when they went near him," she laughed. Grace looked thoughtful for a moment and went on, "he loved fervently and made those things a priority. Like his sister and me. He was so sweet when it came to his sister. But of course, she had him wrapped around her finger." Grace said as she chuckled at the thought of the two of them together.

"Of course she did!" I laughed out loud, "I need to be careful too!"

Grace grinned at me; she could tell that I was already falling for little Elsie. That little girl could turn the hardest of hearts into mush with that sweet smile of hers.

"It was like that from day one with Jaxon. He had taken one look at that little baby girl, and he was smitten. All she ever had to do was ask for anything and he would break his neck to do it." Grace put her hand to her chest as she laughed, "He became her playmate. I can still see all the times he had to play with dolls, have a tea party and the best, was dance party. He especially disliked that one. Poor boy."

I couldn't help but laugh along with Grace. I could just picture a teenage boy having to hold teacups and dance to the latest tunes on the radio. It must have been agony! He had to really love his little sister. I was curious then, "Does Elsie look like Jaxon?"

"No," Grace replied. "Elsie is fairer with her light brown hair like mine and hazel eyes like her fathers. Jaxon had dark hair and clear blue eyes like his father. His real father that is." Grace stumbled over that last statement. She quickly put her hand to her mouth as if she had shared a secret. Then with a sigh she went on, "Charles is not Jaxon's real father. When Jaxon was a baby, we lost his father. That was my first husband, Daniel... my first real loss. The first pain and sorrow inflicted on my heart.

"I met Charles ten years ago when Jaxon was around eight years old. After we dated for a while, Charles asked me to marry him. He told me he wanted to adopt Jaxon, which was truly saying something about his commitment to me. I was so happy that I had found someone who didn't mind a package deal to marry, that I married him and agreed to the adoption." Grace frowned at what she had just said. It was a complex situation, and I was sure she did not want to air all her dirty laundry to me.

Hearing about Jaxon's father passing away, made me a little melancholy. Grace noticed and asked, "Are you all right?"

"I'm sorry, Grace, your story has made me think about my own father. He died when I was a baby too! I never knew much of him other than what my mom has told me. It seems that is something I have in common with your son, Jaxon. The only difference is my mom decided not to replace my father. Instead, she decided to marry her career."

Grace reached out to me and pulled me into her arms. She wrapped her arms around me and held me tightly. "He would have liked you," she whispered.

"If he was anything like you, Grace, I would have liked him too!" I responded softly.

The rest of the afternoon went with ease as conversation flowed naturally between us. When it was time for me to go, she told me to please come back any time.

Chapter 4

I went back to my Aunt Valerie's house with so much on my mind. Grace had been in a desolate place when I arrived, but before I left, she seemed much happier. I was hopeful that my visit brought her some cheer. It was strange to me how I was able to feel the sorrow and pain radiating from Grace when I first arrived turn into a peaceful feeling of emotion. Maybe I had helped! Who knew? It didn't matter how small that help may have been, I just knew it felt good to see Grace smile before I left.

Aunt Valerie had told me that sometimes just being there for someone was a comfort and some help for a person who was grieving. I hoped that's how Grace would feel about me today, I felt the need to be of comfort for her. She had needed someone to talk to about her son that had passed, and I was glad I had been there for her. I went to bed that night feeling good about myself, but the next day, however, would tell a different tale for me.

The next morning, I heard Aunt Valerie sing out to me. "We need to go to town and get your books for summer reading!"

"One more moment!" I called out as I tried to get the brush through the underneath part of my hair. I must have tossed and turned too much last night after my shower; my hair was a rats nest this morning! Getting a brush through it was proving to be difficult.

Quickly I just shoved it into the ponytail band, threw my shoes on and raced down the stairs.

Aunt Valerie was showing me around the town of Cedar Mills. I had not been here in a few years and there definitely had been some changes. I had always liked the downtown main street where we shopped. Cedar Mills took care of their downtown shopping district; I could see the draw. Aunt Val was telling me how they always decorated in themes for the different seasons and holidays. It was adorable! There were little mom and pop stores, like antique, clothing and bookstores. They also had cafés, restaurants and a movie theater. The movie theater also holds live events at the square in the middle of main street. It felt like a scene from a Norman Rockwell painting.

Aunt Val had showed me the new coffee shop that had just opened, and I was thrilled with the thought of a mocha latte! I told her I would run over and get us some latte's while she went to the post office. That way we could take our time sipping our coffee's while meandering our way to the bookstore. I still needed to get the books for my summer reading assignments.

I noticed a few new buildings stood way down at the end of the main street shopping district. I don't remember seeing them before. I asked Aunt Val, "What are those buildings down there?"

She looked in my direction and replied, "That is the new business district. We tore down the old hospital and that big building on the left is the new Cedar Mills Memorial Hospital."

It was a beautifully built hospital with a white brick exterior. It should have been considered a modern building because of the color. However, with the historic architectural features added, the hospital felt like it had always been there in the old town. In fact, all the new buildings of the Cedar Mill business district recently built looked as if they belonged in the old town. It was impressive that the town had grown so much!

Aunt Valerie and I had finished our latte's and were slowly making our way to the bookstore. When she suddenly made the quick decision to go into the Pharmacy for a moment.

Pausing her in midstride, I grabbed her arm asking, "Who is that?!" Nodding my head to the left.

"That my dear, is Grayson Henry Rutherford the Third," she said in an old woman's voice with an English accent. "I guess they liked the name so much they had to use it a third time!"

Aunt Val made me laugh as her accent cracked me up! "Why do you say it like that?"

"Money my dear. Lots of it, but don't set your eyes on that one please. He is nothing but rich-kid trouble. Thinks he owns this whole town; well, his father probably does own half of it, but Grayson has never worked for anything. And in a small town like this, if you are not working hard, you're probably working for trouble!" And with that Aunt Val left me and walked into the Pharmacy.

Wow, did Aunt Val have a terrible opinion of him. Trouble he may be, but easy on the eyes, definitely! I turned my head just a little to slyly get a better look at him. Tall, and athletic looking. He must work out! That shirt he wore was begging for mercy as it stretched across his upper arms and torso. Dark blonde hair with streaks of light blonde running through it. I wondered if this was his natural hair color or was it professionally done? *Probably professional* I snickered to myself.

With a perfect face, nice body, and hair it had me believing that people of wealth were born with superb genes. It just wasn't fair. It's not enough that they were born into wealth, they had to be born beautiful too?!

So deep in thought I was, I neglected to notice that Grayson had been watching me. He caught my eye and smirked at me as if to say, *I know what you're thinking about me.* I felt my face go flush and I quickly looked away. How conceited!

I must have closed my eyes in embarrassment because suddenly I could feel him behind me. Leaning over he whispered in my ear. "You know, you are quite delightful to look at when you are blushing over me".

Oh, dear God! I couldn't breathe. I just stood there like a statue afraid to move. Afraid to open my eyes. When did he move behind me?

However, the venom struck piercing me when he spoke again. "Flattered, but no thanks…. You're not really my type!" I felt the poison spread, stinging me deep, as he walked away.

How dare he! Who the hell does he think he is?! I was furious and began pacing back and forth. *Not his type, am I?* What did he expect? That I would bow down and worship him like every other girl in this town? Did he think I would break down and cry because he did not want me? Oh hell, no! That was never going to happen I determined.

I was still fuming when I saw my Aunt Val walk out of the Pharmacy holding her little bag. She noticed the look of anger and annoyance on my face.

"I'm sorry, was I in there too long? I didn't mean to make you wait."

"NO!" I shouted a little too loudly. She looked at me blinking and I readjusted my attitude. I wasn't mad at her after all. "I mean no, not at all. I'm sorry, I was just deep in thought."

I didn't want to tell her about my little moment with the Almighty Grayson Henry Rutherford the Third. Keeping it a secret to myself I decided to fib a little. "I was just thinking about what my new school was going to be like." This *was* half true. I was worried about my new school. Being the new girl was going to be tough enough, but if I ended up having to face Grayson at school, life was going to be downright miserable!

"Don't let that bother you. You have a whole summer to get ready. Now, let's go get those books you need and get on home. I'm sure Uncle Henry is missing us by now," she smiled.

Bother me? She had no idea what was going to be bothering me.

Chapter 5

I am feeling so miserable. Nowhere to go, and nothing to do. Should I stay in the barn or go back into the house? I hate going into the house, it feels so depressing to me. Seeing my personal things laying there collecting dust is a constant reminder to me that I am gone. *Quit the whining, Jaxon,* I thought to myself. But what is the purpose of keeping everything as it was? My mother is probably keeping it this way as a shrine to me. She is using it as an escape from the reality that I am no longer here. She is lying to herself that I am still around and not gone forever.

Elsie also feels the need to sneak into my bedroom from time to time as well. My little sister sits on the bed staring off into space, sometimes with my pillow in her arms. Elsie and I had a remarkably close relationship, and I am sure she is missing me greatly. It is tough seeing that look of emptiness in their eyes when I catch them in their moments of sadness.

As much as the house is intolerable to me, I feel more relaxed in the barn. The horses are good company to me. I take the opportunity to talk to them whenever I am able. Of course, they are not much for conversation. Whether they understand me or not is another thing; the horses tend to respond to me with a nod or a neigh.

They say animals are highly attuned to the spirit world of which I am now residing. Recently, I have been trying my hand at manifesting, materializing into a figure. I find it difficult, and it takes a lot of energy out of me; but I feel the horses sense I am here.

I am unsure if anyone can see me in my manifested form. It's not like there are any rule books to read or videos to watch in Purgatory that would give me information about my existence. For now, I just need to make sure I stay unseen. The last thing I need around here is a bunch of ghosthunters and fake psychics trying to prove my existence. I don't need any proof of that ... I know I am here.

She appeared as I was in the middle of pulling my energy together to manifest. I stopped. Who is this girl walking into the barn? Taking a moment, I observed her as she made her way around the barn inspecting it and the horses too. She was beautiful! Her energy was bright and strong, and I could tell by her demeanor that she did not know how beautiful she truly was.

She walked over to the horse closest to her. It was Grey, the horse that had belonged to me. He is a large quarter horse that I rode around on the farm. He is a feisty animal though and would only let me ride him; no one else could seem to get near him.

Watching her gently lift her hand, she paused, allowing the horse to sense she meant no harm. I was truly concerned for her safety. Grey can be temperamental, and I didn't want this beautiful girl to get hurt. To my surprise, Grey bowed his head in approval, as she rubbed his nose, sliding her hand up and behind his ear lightly scratching. I couldn't believe it! Grey's submission to this girl is a surprise to me. I could tell that the horse was loving the affection she was giving him. Laughing to myself, I was thinking about how much I would have loved it too.

Getting lost in the scene playing out in front of me, I absent-mindedly moved over to the other side of the stall trying to get a closer look. As I moved, a crash sounded. I froze! I had tipped one of the grooming brushes over, making it fall inside a bucket.

"Who's there?!" The girl cried out. The hair on her arms must have raised. She began rubbing her arms up and down. She looked around to see if someone was in the barn with her. God, I felt like an idiot! How could I make such a loud noise when I was trying to hide from people?

The girl stood silently still next to the horse, letting her eyes scan the barn. Grey started whinnying and pacing in his stall. The girl began talking to him, "Shh, shh, shh, it's okay, I'll check it out." She spoke gently to the horse. She walked around the barn to the other stalls, checking where the other two horses stood. She inspected the area looking for the reason for a crash. Nothing! I knew she would find nothing. She walked to the other three empty stalls and glanced around and still saw nothing. She reached the empty stall I was in and peered over the railing. In the corner she noticed the grooming brush haphazardly sitting in a bucket.

The girl laughed to herself "I must be losing it!" She walked back over to Grey, petting him while she said "We are silly to have been so spooked! It was probably a field mouse or some other small animal that made the brush fall into the bucket." With one last look around the barn, satisfied that no one was there, she left.

I blew out a slow sigh trying to calm my own nerves and walked back over to where Grey was pacing. I decided to go back to practicing my manifesting. Pulling together as much energy as I could, I became a physical form. Reaching out to the horse, I spoke at the same time, saying "Hey there, big fellow … it's just me, Jaxon. You know me, it's okay, let's calm down." At that moment, Grey suddenly stood still. I was stunned. I spoke again to the horse, saying, "You feel me, don't you, boy?!" The horse turned his head as if he understood everything I had just said and stared right into my eyes. *Oh God*, I thought to myself, *I did it! He sees me*!

Chapter 6

I was meeting Grace today for a short visit. No one else was home and that always seemed the time she would call. She handed me a glass of iced tea and a slice of her cake, something I couldn't turn down. We spent the afternoon talking and laughing over Elsie's escapades. After a while, I could tell there was something pressing on her mind. Not wanting to make it hard on her, I decided to ask, "Grace is there something you wanted to ask me?"

Grace looked at me with surprise in her eyes, "Alisa, how did you know?"

"You have this look of apprehension on your face," I laughed.

Looking guilty, her face flushed. "I wanted to ask if you would you be interested in watching Elsie for us from time to time?"

As if I would ever turn that down! I loved Elsie. Without hesitation, I responded "Absolutely! When do you need me?"

She looked at me and relief was written all over her face. "We have some functions coming up with our church and a couple of small overnight trips that we have to take for farming business. Normally I wouldn't go, but Charles thought it would be a good idea for me to get away since I am so comfortable with the idea of you taking care of Elsie."

Wait … did she say Charles thought it was a good idea? I was struck that she said Charles. Was he showing care and concern for Grace? All the times I have been here and experienced his tongue lashings, he was not the most pleasant of people to say the least. But it humbled me that Grace had enough confidence in me to stay with Elsie. Plus, I'm sure she knew that I could always call my aunt and uncle across the road if there was a problem. They could be here in seconds.

I was getting ready to leave, when I saw a young man walking down the long driveway. "Who is that?" I asked.

Grace looked up and sighed. "That's Roger West. He lives down the road a bit. Nice kid, but a little slow of the mind. He's not able to work a regular job, so, Charles and I let him help around the farm as a way to make a bit of money when we're able."

He made his way to the front porch and stopped. "Hi, Ms. Hanley." He smiled at her.

"Hello Roger, I wasn't expecting you. What brings you here today?"

"I wasn't doing nothing, so I came to see you. Just wonderin' if you needed me to help you today." His eyes shone with excitement as he spoke to Grace.

Shaking her head, no, Grace spoke gently to him. "I'm sorry, Roger, Mr. Hanley has it under control. We don't have anything for you to do around here today."

Roger looked dejected when Grace turned him down. "Who's this?" he asked pointing in my direction.

"This is our friend, Alisa"

Roger looked at me with a look of confusion on his face. So, I decided to speak up, "Hi Roger, I'm new to the area. I li ....." I saw Grace quickly shake her head NO! As if to say, do not tell him where you live. I caught the hint and changed what I was going to say, "I ... I mean where do you live?"

"Over there," he pointed down the road, which I assumed was a couple of farms over. He eyed me again and said, "You sure are pretty."

Well, that was a bit random. And a little uncomfortable. Feeling the uneasiness between Grace and Roger, I decided to ignore the comment with a "Thank you." Grace was the savior of the conversation and told Roger that he could come back the next day. Maybe Mr. Hanley would have some work for him to do then. I noticed she never gave the impression that her husband was not at home. Roger seemed satisfied with her answer and left for home.

I looked at Grace and asked, "You say he is challenged - what happened?" I asked trying to be sensitive with my questioning.

"Roger was in middle school when he had a silo accident. He fell into the silo filled with some feed. His father saw him fall in and was able to dig him out. Unfortunately, he basically suffocated while he was in there. The EMT's were able to resuscitate him, but he had been without oxygen a little too long. This caused some damage to the brain. He was in the hospital for quite a while doing rehab and learning how to do everyday things again. He has come a long way and is much better now."

"That is so sad!" I immediately felt sorry for him, even though I got a creepy vibe from him. Reflecting on the conversation we had just held with Roger, I asked, "Why did you shake your head no when I was going to tell him where I live?"

"Saving you, your aunt and uncle some aggravation. He means well, but he would start showing up at your house all the time. We made that mistake of befriending him and well, as you can see, he feels he can show up anytime he likes. If I am here alone, I usually do not answer the door."

"Thank you for saving me!" I chuckled. We continued our conversation until she thought Roger was long gone and felt safe enough for me to go home. What a strange afternoon this was turning out to be. First, the unexplained noise in the barn and the feeling that I was not alone spooked me a little. Second, Grace telling me about Charles being a comfort and now this Roger character! My head was spinning with everything that had taken place and I took my time walking home trying to make sense of it all.

Aunt Valerie was waiting for me when I made it home. It was close to her dinner time, and I had to be honest, I was far from hungry. Grace had fed me some of her cake and I was still full.

"How did your visit go?" She asked.

"Great! Grace asked me if I would like to babysit for them."

"What did you tell her?"

"Of course, I said yes! I love little Elsie and I could definitely use a part time job. She even said there would be some business trips that would require me to stay overnight. I think Grace thought I would be a good fit, since you are right here if I had any trouble."

"I agree! You know I am right here if you need me for anything. Now go get cleaned up and get ready for dinner."

"Already?!"

Aunt Val eyed me suspiciously, "She fed you, didn't she?"

I laughed, "It was only a piece of cake!"

"Go run around the house or something. Work it off so you can eat dinner with me and your uncle."

"Yes Ma'am!" I saluted her and took a quick run up the road and back. I didn't think it was going to do me much good, but I would stuff whatever I could into me to satisfy her.

Later that night as I settled in for the evening in my room, I called my mom and Nikki. I missed both of them terribly and wanted to tell them about my stories from today. I needed that connection I was missing while staying here. Feeling a little melancholy, I had to admit I was feeling a little lonely here.

When I called Nikki, she laughed at me, of course when I relayed my "spooky barn" story. She agreed with me that it was probably a small animal and nothing more even though I could swear I had felt a presence in the barn.

Mom on the other hand advised I stay away from Roger during my phone call with her. She seemed happy for me that Grace asked me to babysit for them. It was sounding like a part-time job which is something I was looking for. "And you can't beat the commute!" she added. I had to laugh in agreement with her. Man, I missed my mom and couldn't wait for her to come home.

Chapter 7

A few days later I was back at the Hanley Farm to babysit Elsie. She seemed just as excited about me coming over as I was to watch her. Charles and Grace left with explicit instructions on the do's and don'ts for watching their daughter. They would be back by nightfall, and I was to help myself to the refrigerator for lunch and dinner with Elsie.

This was my first time getting a full tour of the house, and I tried not to show how eager I was. Grace walked me around, showing me all the historic details, she knew I had wanted to see. When the tour was over, she gave Elsie a quick hug telling her to behave for me and left with Charles.

I decided it would be a perfect day to pack a lunch and take Elsie on a trek to the northwest side of the farm where the trees were closest. We watched ourselves as we walked around the crops and used a path that led into the woods. Elsie was excited to go off and explore and it was contagious, and I was getting eager to go too.

"You know, my brother used to take me explornin'!" She grinned her toothless smile at me.

"You mean exploring," I corrected her.

"Yeah, that too! He used to make up stories on the way and we would play them out. Like pirates looking for lost treasure or secret agents trying to spy and not get caught by the bad guys. It was sooooooo fun! Can you tell stories like that?"

"It does sound like fun, but I'm not that great at storytelling. I can, however, show you how to make stuff with things in the woods."

"Really?! That sounds neat too!"

We made our way into the woods and came across a stream. This would be the perfect place to have lunch and play. I spread out an old blanket I had found in the barn, and we set up our lunch. As we ate, I pointed out all the things in the woods that I knew about. Trees, wild mushrooms, berries, moss, birds. After eating, I showed her how to make moss huts with sticks and we found pretty rocks in the stream to use for pathways. We ended up making a small village and Elsie was proud of what we had accomplished. After playing a bit longer, I noticed that Elsie was slowing down and getting tired. By the time we reached the house, we were both exhausted.

"I'm beat, Elsie! How about we take a nap for a few minutes?"

"Naps are for babies," she said scrunching her face up at me.

"Okay, how about we call it resting then? Let's just rest for a few minutes," I said smiling down at her. She seemed to like that better and went to her room to lay down. I decided to lay down on the couch. I was so tired from the walk, the heat, and entertaining Elsie that I drifted off almost immediately.

I started dreaming. It was a beautiful day outside, the sun shone and there was a nice gentle breeze blowing against my face. I looked down and noticed I was dressed in eighteenth century attire, the same era as the house. I was out on the long driveway walking towards the house with my long skirt swinging and I held a parasol to shade me from the sun. The breeze stopped and it became stifling hot while I walked, and I began to sweat profusely. Sweating was not dignified! I made my way to the porch and tried to maintain my composure.

I decided to take a moment and sit in one of the rocking chairs on the front porch. I looked to my right and a glass of lemonade was sitting on the table next to me. Relief swept through me as I picked up the glass and sipped the lemonade while fanning myself, trying to keep cool. I wondered how the lemonade was provided to me because there was no one else around.

I set the glass back onto the table next to me and suddenly, the dream changed. I felt a cold blast of air to the left side of me as the front door to the house slammed open. The heat that had been choking me dissipated when I was enveloped into the house. Time shifting forward, I was back in my shorts and t-shirt standing in what I assumed to be the living room. I saw the outline of the windows and couch before the room started turning dark.

The blackness was encroaching me, and I could no longer see. With my arms outstretched, I used my hands to feel my way as I slowly moved forward trying to find the couch. I wanted to so sit down. I needed to feel safe, and I wanted to have some security underneath me. I was scared and unsure as to what the dark in this room wanted from me. It had a presence about it.

It was getting colder and colder by the minute. So cold I could have probably seen my exhaled breath if there was any light, but there was none to be had. Finally, I found the couch as the darkness seemed to surround me moving in closer. I tried pushing back into the couch trying to shrink away from it. "What do you want from me?" I called out. A deafening silence was the response, so silent it hurt my ears.

Shivers ran down my spine as I fought to adjust my sight, but the darkness was too thick to see through. Frightened, I lay down and curled into a ball, folding into myself to get some warmth. I was racked with fear as the silence, cold and darkness became intense, the air thickened, and I could barely breathe. A moment later, I felt an ice-cold touch on my face, tracing up my cheek, and encircling my ear. I gasped and my eyes flew open as I jolted awake in a panic.

What ... the hell ... was that?!! I was not one to have bad dreams. Especially not in the middle of the day. I shivered again with the memory of the dream that had just transpired. I put my fingers to the place on my face where it had been touched in my dream. It was still slightly cool compared to the rest of my face.

I shook my head from its wooziness and slowly stood up. Feeling light-headed from the panic I had just experienced; I took a moment before walking upstairs. I needed to check on Elsie. I wanted to make sure that she was all right. I ran upstairs and quietly tiptoed down the hall to her door. I peeked into her room, and she was bundled up fast asleep in her bed. The clock on the wall said I had only been asleep for twenty minutes! I closed the door gently and walked back downstairs.

Meandering back into the family room where the television was, I turned it on. As I looked around the room, it felt comfortable to me. There is a coziness about the large brick fireplace and the thick white mantle. Floor to ceiling white bookcases flanked each side of the fireplace. Grace had selected an oversized couch, with colorful pillows and wing back chairs to fill the space.

With the television running in the background, I barely paid attention to it. My eye caught the family photos on the fireplace mantle. The center picture was one of Grace and Charles. This picture must have been taken on their wedding day. Grace looked so beautiful and happy; Charles was an incredibly lucky man. I did not know how Grace could put up with him and his harsh personality. He definitely had no problem taking his wrath out on those around him. There were pictures of Elsie on each side of the wedding photo. Baby pictures, school age pictures, she was utterly adorable.

Off to the left side of the mantle on the bookcase stood a picture that took my breath away. This had to be Grace's son Jaxon in this graduation photo. These pictures were usually taken in the summer before senior year, and I had taken mine before I moved here. Jaxon was wearing the typical black jacket, white shirt and bowtie. His tanned complexion was set off by the white shirt. Grace had described him briefly to me, but she was not even close to this!

I grabbed the photograph and held it for a moment, studying it. Those eyes, piercing blue. You could almost see through them; the blue was so clear. Dark ruffled hair with streaks of auburn and gold running through it. Probably from the sun, I could guarantee that his highlights did not come out of a bottle. His nose was straight and his jaw line sharp, but what melted me was that smile. That smile led its way to the dimples in his cheeks.

His face was hard, but the sweetness of the dimples tamed him. I could tell he was full of confidence. It was in his eyes and his smile had the look of prankster there. God, I would have given anything to have met him. Of course, I probably would have been on a long list of girls that would have wanted to be with Jaxon.

"I bet you had the pick of the litter with looks like that!" I said aloud. I felt a blast of coldness as I put the picture back on the bookcase. I rubbed my arms up and down to put warmth back into them. Must be a vent somewhere blowing the air conditioning on me.

I sat down on the sofa to watch television, but I could not focus on it. My mind was too busy memorizing that picture of Jaxon. I kept running his face over and over in my mind. I kept glancing back at Jaxon's photo. I felt heartbroken; *why did he have to be gone?* Was it possible to have a crush on a photograph? I had to laugh at myself. Had I truly gone nuts? It was ridiculous, but he was just so beautiful to look at. If you could say that a guy was beautiful.

"I bet you had the world on a silver platter, Mr. Jaxon," I muttered. Looks like that, made life easier it seemed.

"Huh!" I heard a gruff voice whispering from behind me.

I turned my head quickly to look. I felt a prickling go up my spine, sensing a presence in the room, but no one was there. Of course, there was no one here,

I was alone. Unless Elsie finally got up from her nap. I decided to check things out and went on upstairs. Elsie was just waking and getting out of her bed. "Well, that answered that question," I muttered to myself. *Must have been the television.* I was hardly paying attention to it anyway.

The rest of the evening went without incident. Elsie and I had fun playing some more, ate dinner and then went out to the barn to feed the horses when the Hanleys arrived. Grace insisted that Charles drive me home since it was dark outside. It would be a little awkward being alone with him since we had never talked when I visited. At the end of the driveway before crossing the road, he saw headlights coming from his left that proceeded to fly by at a high rate of speed.

"Damn crazy kids! Think they are the only ones on the roads these days. Imagine if we had let you walk on home? Why, you could have been hit, killed even!" He complained.

I was shocked, this was the most Charles had spoken to me. Ever. I didn't think he had a concerned bone in his body, never mind worrying about me of all people. "Do they do this often?" I asked.

"Every now and then … especially on a Friday or Saturday night. They like to use this road as a dragstrip, racing each other. Ask your aunt and uncle, I bet they don't want you walking across this road at night either."

I thanked him for driving me home and went on into the house.

"Did everything go okay today?" Aunt Val called out.

"All things good! But I'm exhausted." I heard Aunt Val chuckle as she said something about little kids while I walked on up to my room to get ready for bed. I decided to skip my nightly call with Nikki. I was exhausted and my mind was brimming with the memories from today. Maybe I had overdone it with the walk to the stream and keeping Elsie so entertained, or maybe it was that weird dream. I couldn't get that dream out of my mind, it freaked me out, and I swore I heard a voice in the family room tonight. There was nobody there but me and the television … it had to be the TV. Instead of filling my subconscious with these bad deliberations, I decided to meditate on that picture of Jaxon. With his face swirling in my mind, I fell into a blissful sleep.

Chapter 8

A few days later, I called out to Aunt Valerie. "My turn to go over to Grace's house!"

"O ... kay ... I was over there yesterday. Is she expecting you?"

"Yes ma'am. She wants to show me some hidden features built into the house that she knew I would like to see. She knows how much I love that old house and all the history behind it."

"Well, that sounds amazing! Have a wonderful time."

"Will do, and I'll be back before supper time," I said as I waltzed out the door. I was thinking about Jaxon's picture. Grace had described him to me, but words did not do him justice. I thought of him as I blew out a calming breath. I wanted to look at his picture again. I needed to see that face; I was drawn to it. So beautiful. I know that is a bizarre thing to say about a guy, but it was true. I found myself at the edge of our property and after my conversation with Charles last night, I decided to look before crossing the road. A car was coming and knew I should wait for it to pass. As it approached, I heard the brakes abruptly hit and the wheels screeched to a stop. The window rolled down and there sitting in front of me was my tormentor ... Grayson Henry Rutherford the Third.

"Well, hello there, luscious," he said in a snarky voice, looking me up and down like he was appraising a statue.

"I am not responding to you and your silly characterizations. I'm very busy and need to get going," I said in the haughtiest voice I could muster. This seemed to do nothing but amuse Grayson and he smiled a rather large smile. God, those teeth were perfect; I hated him.

"Are you living here? I can assume you do. Now I know where to call on you when I need a visit."

"You cannot and will not *'call on me'* at any time. Besides, when you last spoke to me, I was ... and I quote ... not your type!"

Grayson laughed out loud; I had fallen right into his trap of provocation. He turned his head back at me and gave me his mocking smile and winked at me. "I guess I left you with thoughts of me on your mind after all."

"It's always a game to you, isn't it?" I huffed.

"No, not at all," he said sarcastically. "I love the thought of being on *your* mind, it makes my job easier. Besides, I can get any girl I want to fall for me. You want to be with me too. You just won't admit it yet."

"Oh no, NOT this girl ... and you can best remember that! Now please get out of my way, I have things to do."

"Hmmm, you better be careful my sweets, I do love a good challenge," he said and sped off down the road.

The nerve of him! As if I would ever remotely consider going out with him or have any kind of relationship with him. So arrogant and uncaring of how he makes other people feel. I have no use for people like that in my life. I liked to think I was a nice person ... and nice people don't always have to finish last!

Finding myself running down the long driveway to Grace's house, had me feeling good. I needed to run more often; I was missing it. I had been so busy lately helping around my aunt and uncle's farm, summer reading, and coming here to Grace's house. I had neglected to do the one thing that I loved. I decided I would run on the way home and maybe run down the road too. Stretch my legs out, as some would call it.

Grace and I had a nice visit that day. She showed me things that I had not seen before, like the butler's pantry and the old pocket doors that slide into the walls when not in use. She even showed me a secret pass-through built in a china cupboard in the dining room that opened into the kitchen. Someone had closed it up and it wasn't being used, so she had Charles reopen it. It was fascinating! I could just imagine what it must have been like living here well over a hundred years ago when the house was first built. It was so beautiful.

The property and the house had been in Grace's family since it was built, and she had inherited it. The feeling of the house played on my senses. Standing in this home, I was getting a feeling of warmth and nostalgia, along with a little feeling of mystery and uneasiness. A very odd mix of sensations. But if Grace and Elsie were comfortable in this old house, I was good with that.

After Grace and I had our visit, I played with Elsie for a few minutes. Before I left, I asked if I could go and pet the horses again today. I told Grace about my visit with Grey the quarter horse, and how he was my favorite. Her face brightened. "That was Jaxon's horse; he loved Grey! Go on to the barn and take your time. I'll see you tomorrow, right?" she said.

"Absolutely, I will be here to watch Elsie, 5:00 p.m. on the dot."

"Thank you so much, Alisa. You have become a tremendous help to us."

"Trust me, Grace, the pleasure is all mine. I am in love with Elsie!"

That made her smile as she went on into the house and I walked over to the barn. Charles was way out in the fields working, while Elsie played in the house with Grace. I took advantage of this time to be alone in the barn. I liked it here. The smell of hay, wood and horses were comforting to me. I looked around in amazement noticing this place was spotless; actually, the Hanleys kept everything spotless! The stalls were freshly mucked, and horses brushed down.

I wondered how Charles was able to get everything done while he worked the acres and acres of crops. Then I remembered … oh yes, Roger. I frowned at the thought of him and the way he made me a little uncomfortable. Not because of his mental handicap but because of the way he hassled the Hanleys. I was glad Grace had stopped me from telling Roger where I lived. That would have been a disaster if he started hanging around our place constantly. Poor guy, I kind of felt sorry for him and wondered what type of home life he had. I hoped they were nice to him and gave him a good home.

I was deep in thought when I entered the barn. For a split second, I thought I had seen a figure in the back corner. I held my breath in and stood quietly for a second as I scanned the barn. Should I investigate? It would be foolish to put myself in danger if someone was here. I felt the need to check it out and went ahead to look around the back of the barn. I looked high, low and behind things but did not see anything. Funny, I still felt as if someone were here.

Suddenly a cold wind rushed right through me, and that sense of a presence dissipated. I shivered and crossed my arms to rub them up and down, bringing heat to my body. That was the second time something strange had happened out here. I knew I should leave or go tell Grace, but I was drawn to this mystery; I wanted to figure this out. *That must be the teenager in me,* I laughed to myself.

I spoke to Grey and petted him before I left. He must like me as well, since he bent his head down to nuzzle my neck. Such a sweet thing. "You're such a good boy, Grey, maybe I will be able to ride you someday." As if he understood he bristled and shook his head up and down. Deciding to leave, I remembered that I wanted to take a run.

I ran down the long driveway and turned to my right to run down Ash Fort Road. I remembered what Charles had said about the cars, so I kept a vigil on looking out for them. God, I needed this, it felt wonderful and freeing. My mind started to open and all my thoughts and emotions that were pent up began rolling out. Letting everything go, working through the excess energy my body was using, my mind was clearer than it had been in a while. I was pretty far down the road when I realized I needed to turn around and go on back home.

Looking to my right, I saw a cute farmhouse sitting back into a field. *Wow, it seems there are nothing but farms here.* This one was smaller than my aunt and uncle's and way smaller than the Hanley farm. I saw a figure of a young man feeding pigs, throwing what I would assume to be slop into a trough. He looked up and saw me with recognition in his eyes. I realized it was Roger. He threw his bucket down and waved starting to walk towards the road. I decided it was not a good idea to encourage him, remembering Grace's warning, so I nodded to him and turned quickly, taking off back down the road to my family's farm. I knew it would be tough to sprint after running for so long, but I was not going to let myself get into harm's way.

"Alisa, Alisa … wait! I only want to say hi. Don't leave. Come back!"

I felt guilty but pretended not to hear him calling out to me. By the time he got to the end of his driveway my hope was that I would be far enough away that he would not follow me. I kept sprinting and my lungs were burning. I did a quick glance back and saw that Roger was not running after me.

"Thank God," I muttered to myself as I blew out a slow breath. I must have been seized up in fear and now felt a sense of relief run through my body as I slowed down to a light jog. I walked the last few feet and took the time to stretch out my limbs. My body screamed at me while my feet were on fire. The evasion from Roger left me completely spent. I went upstairs to take a long hot shower and got ready for a nice quiet evening with Aunt Val and Uncle H. Maybe I would call and talk to my mom tonight; it was days like today that I missed her greatly.

Chapter 9

The next evening, I was scheduled to babysit for Grace. This was becoming my part-time job and I was thrilled because of how much I loved Elsie! Best job I've ever had … if you want to call it a job. I almost felt guilty letting Grace and Charles pay me to watch her. I was having way too much fun. That night we decided to play with the horses, then watch a movie after dinner. By 8:30 that evening, Elsie was done. Completely exhausted from the great outdoors. You gotta love fresh air! I made sure she washed up and put her to bed, reading a story to her until she fell asleep. That did not take long, I laughed to myself.

Pulling the door closed as I was leaving her room, I stood in the hall for a moment. Waiting to hear if she was going to attempt to sneak out of bed. I knew she was worn out, but I wanted to make sure.

As I stood there, I looked at the door at the end of the hall with band stickers on it. This must have been Jaxon's room and I felt curious to go and check the room out. Quietly I tip-toed down the hall and paused before opening the door. *To enter or not to enter* … I was literally fighting with myself. Was it considered an invasion of privacy if I went in there? Well, Jaxon was not here to ask if I could go into his room. But I would not want Grace to be upset with me either.

Curiosity made the decision for me. Turning the knob of the door, I pushed gently. Taking a quick look back at Elsie's door, I made sure she didn't hear anything and get up. Satisfied that I couldn't hear any noises from her room, I walked into Jaxon's room and softly shut the door behind me. Standing there in the dark before I could turn on the light, the hair on my arms raised. Somebody is in this room; I can feel it! Did someone break in while we were in the barn? Was it Roger? God, I hoped not.

I was beyond scared, and my mind raced thinking about what I should do. If someone were in this room, they surely would have seen me by now. Maybe they were hiding and were waiting for me to make the first move. Thinking of Elsie's safety as well as my own, I knew I couldn't just run away. Out of the corner of my eye I saw the outline of a baseball bat leaning against the bookcase next to the door I had just shut. Shifting my weight to my left I reached over and slowly picked up the baseball bat. I knew this was a very dumb idea. All the self-defense in Physical Education class had told me to never confront danger but try and find a way to get away from it. If someone were in this room, they already had the advantage, since I entered the room after they did.

With the baseball bat in my hands, I quickly raised it up and demanded, "Who's there?! I know there is someone here, SHOW YOURSELF!"

"NO!" said a harsh male voice, as if I had interrupted something important.

A coldness whooshed through me sending me backwards into the door. *IT WENT THROUGH ME!!* I screamed internally, feeling dizzy and breathless. I needed to sit down. Lowering the bat, I felt for the light switch on the wall and turned it on. No longer could I sense the presence that was here when I first entered the room. I decided to check all the windows, the closet and under the bed before I sat down. Nothing! There is nothing here! I sat down on the bed for a moment and calmed myself down. I knew I had heard something and definitely had just felt something go through me. I needed to relax and stop letting my mind get the best of me.

I still had the goosebumps and could not get that chill out of my system. There is something happening here. This was another strange experience I could add to my list, and I was getting very suspicious. I started to think there was a ghost in this house, not that I believed in things such as ghosts, or spirits as some would call them. I had never faced anything like this before and wondered if Grace has ever felt or experienced anything in this house. Rolling my eyes, I wondered how I would even approach the subject. *"Excuse me Grace, did you know you had ghosts running around in your house?"* Ridiculous! I rubbed my arms up and down again and looked around the room.

It was a typical teenage boy's room. The sneakers in the corner looked like they had just been kicked off. A desk, band posters on the wall ... some were from the seventies and eighties era, nice. I liked music from that time-period too. In the corner of the room, I saw a vintage stereo system with all kinds of records and CD's, "Now that is very cool!" I whispered. As I stood there checking out all the music, I heard creaking of the floors in the hallway.

Someone seemed to be walking back and forth, like they were pacing.

"Crap, Elsie is out of bed!" I quickly turned off the light to Jaxon's room. I didn't know how she would react to me being in here and I did not want to upset her. Quietly, I opened the door to Jaxon's room, slipped out into the hall and shut the door behind me. The hall was dark and quiet. Elsie was nowhere to be found. I walked to Elsie's room and opened the door just enough to peek in and saw that she was still in her bed fast asleep.

"I am losing my damn mind!" I mumbled as I closed the door. Deciding to forego any further investigations upstairs, I went downstairs to watch TV while I waited for Grace and Charles to arrive home. Turning on the television, I decided to go and look at Jaxon's picture again and studied it. I had to really stop doing this. I was drawn to his picture and addicted to that face. I was taking every opportunity to get a peek at it whenever I came over. This time I didn't take it off the bookshelf. *Well, that is progress,* I thought shaking my head at my own silliness.

Not wanting to fall asleep, I decided to sit down and try to watch the television. The last time I fell asleep her, I had that weird nightmare. Pure madness! It took me a few days to get over that one, I still swear it felt real. Something had touched my face that afternoon while I slept, I just know it! *Don't even think about it,* I told myself. I did not need any reminders of that creep fest. Boy, would I have plenty to tell Nikki tonight when we talked later.

Chapter 10

Grace had told me to swing by today since Charles had taken Elsie to town. It was cool, because I wanted to go back and see Grey the quarter horse too. He had me smitten! He gets so excited to see me that he nuzzles me all the time when I visit. Probably because I like to bring him treats! I rounded the corner to the entrance of the barn and stiffened. My spine tingled and once again the hair on my arms rose and I could feel somebody. Was it Roger? I didn't want to go in if he was in there. I don't know why, but he really gave me the creeps. I stealthily moved closer to the door and listened for movement. I heard nothing. I must be imagining things now and decided to go on into the barn to see Grey. I heard him whinnying. That was not like him since he was usually very calm. Something in there had upset him.

I kept my vigil and heard a low voice speaking to Grey, trying to keep him calm. The horse seemed to change his demeanor and bristled in agreement to whomever was speaking. Curious, I walked in to see who was talking to the horse and screamed out loud. A familiar pair of eyes were looking right at me. *It couldn't be! It's not possible!* I wanted to run, but my feet would not budge. *Go, just go* I thought to myself, I wanted to speak but could no longer find my voice after screaming.

Standing there, I waited for my mind to unfreeze and catch up with my body. I couldn't decide if I should run or even which way I should run. I moved right, then left when I heard, "Please don't go." I shook my head, closed my eyes, and reopened them to make sure I was really seeing what was in front of me. It was Jaxon Harrison Hanley!

He held up his hands to show he meant no harm. I knew in my heart he would not hurt me. But the fact that he was here, and I could see him, made me speechless. His eyes met mine and he looked pained as if my reaction were causing him sorrow. While his hands were up facing me, he said, "Please don't run away from me. I didn't know you would be able to see me, and I don't want you to be fearful of me."

"I ... I'm not afraid of you," I said finally finding my voice. "I'm just surprised that you are here. Standing in front of me. How is this possible? You do know that you're dead, right? I mean I should not be seeing you, right?! God that sounded terrible ... I did not mean it the way it sounded. I'm Alisa, by the way." *Would you just shut up Alisa!* My nerves were letting my mouth run away and I felt guilty stating that he was dead, but I wanted to make sure he knew.

"Of course, I know I'm dead." Jaxon stated cynically. Then he changed his tone to not offend me. "Wait, you know who I am?"

"Of course! I would recognize your face anywhere. Your mother has told me all about you, plus I saw your picture in the family room." Now, I was fascinated. How many times had I dreamed of talking to Jaxon and getting to know him? I would have given anything to be near him and now here he was, standing in front of me. I had to know, "How are you so ... formed?"

"Manifested," he said and stopped. "I'm sorry. Can we talk about something else? I see you around here all the time and I'm really surprised that you can see me." Jaxon said as he lowered his arms. "There have been times when I was close to you ... so close, I wondered if you could feel me."

Feeling more at ease, I took a few steps further into the barn as I answered him. "I think I did. When you are near me, it's the coldness that I feel, yes?"

"Yes ... my mom, my sister ... everyone seems immune to me when I am around. I could tell you felt something. I wanted to let you know it was me but was afraid of frightening you. Are you afraid now?"

"Why would I be afraid, Jaxon? I mean this is crazy, right? Maybe I am crazy now, but I sense you do not intend to hurt me."

"I'm so glad you feel that way. And no, you are not crazy. This is really happening." He gave me a smile showing me his dimples.

I was rocked to my core; his face made my heart hurt. Were my dreams coming true right before my very eyes? I had studied the picture of his face so many times and here I was talking to him.

"The first time I saw you in the barn, you were with Grey here. I was watching, and I accidentally knocked over the grooming brush into the bucket."

"I thought I felt a presence, and decided it was a small animal!" I laughed.

"I also found you asleep on the couch in our house, and I just had to touch you. I hope you don't mind that I did that."

"That was you?" I touched my cheek with the memory of it. "I knew I was not imagining things."

He smiled shyly as he continued his story. "Yes, that was me. I could not resist; you were sleeping so peacefully."

"That afternoon I felt my cheek after I awoke, and it was so cold."

"It has only been recently, that I decided to learn how to manifest. I haven't perfected it one hundred percent, but I am close."

"Are you able to feel things? Like, with your hands in this state?"

"Grey here lets me pet him, don't you boy." He petted Grey on the nose and Grey nuzzled closer to Jaxon. "He doesn't seem to be afraid, nor does he mind the coldness of my hands."

"Can … I know this is going to sound weird, but can I touch your hand?" I wanted to see if it was solid or cold. I had this need to feel Jaxon … wait, *pump the breaks, Alisa, you are talking about a ghost!* I didn't care though; I could not explain it. It was almost as if he were a magnet pulling at me, at my soul, and I could not get close enough.

Jaxon looked a little shy at that moment, with his eyes lowered he said, "Yes" in a near whisper.

I paused before walking towards him. Was he feeling the same way? Was he as drawn to me as I was to him? I held these thoughts in my mind as I walked over towards him and held my hand out to him. He raised his hand and touched mine. It was cold, but it felt real. Almost like a human's touch, but not as firm. Like he said, he wasn't one hundred percent there.

I was curious to know if he could feel me in the same manner. Turning my hand over I traced my fingers over his hand. I felt sorry for him, knowing it had been a long time since he had actual human contact. "Do you feel me when I touch you too Jaxon?"

"Yes," he said softly, closing his eyes as if he was relishing my touch. "God, you do not know how long I have needed this, to feel another humans touch. I thought I would have to walk this world alone in silence without a person's touch or interactions. This feels so unreal to me, you do not know how miserable I have been this past year. Trying to get used to this world I live in, which I loathe, by the way."

"I thought that you go to heaven or hell when you die. At least that is what I have always been told."

Jaxon sighed and shook his head. "That is usually the case. Unless someone is keeping you here, binding you by their grief."

"You mean Grace?!" I asked in surprise. Jaxon nodded yes. I knew she would be devastated to know that her son was tied here due to her grief over him. She would never forgive herself.

"If you can talk to me, Jaxon, why don't you just talk to her and ask her to release you?"

"It doesn't work that way, believe me! I have tried many times to get her to notice me or react to me. Besides it's against the rules of *my* purgatory. Can't go to heaven. Can't go to hell, not that I would want to go to hell. No, I guess I'll just walk this damned farm for eternity, it seems." He spewed the words as if they were poison.

"Do you want me to talk to her for you?" I asked carefully, not wanting to upset him any further. I didn't want him to leave yet.

"No, you can't! That's against the rules too. Hell, you're not even supposed to see me or be able to talk to me. I am not sure how this is happening unless you have a gift for the spirit world. Grey here can see me; actually, all animals can see me. They have what you might call a sixth sense or a mind's eye."

I decided to forego my visit with Grace today and stay in the barn with Jaxon. It was obvious he had been thirsty for conversation. We ended up sitting in the corner of the barn talking and talking for a long while. It was time we spent learning more about each other, until it became clear he was exhausted. It took a lot of energy for him to stay in a manifested form. He was getting ready to leave me, when he stopped and looked at me, reaching out he touched my face. "So beautiful," he said and disappeared.

Chapter 11

Dumbfounded ... That is how he left me. I was standing there lost in a world of elation. My mind was running a hundred miles an hour, completely bewildered by what had just transpired. It took me a moment to get my thoughts together, knowing I had to leave. When I finally snapped back to reality, I found myself racing home. I couldn't seem to get home fast enough, thinking about what I had just witnessed. I ran upstairs to my room needing to be alone and give myself the time to process what I had experienced.

Jaxon had revealed himself to me and confided in me the secrets about his "rules" of death. Was this real? Did it really happen? I hoped it wasn't just a figment of my imagination. I sat down at my desk and turned on my computer, curious to see if I could find out anything regarding the spirit world. Most of the information was from non-believers, stating that ghosts or spirits did not exist. However, I learned that fifty percent of the population believe in ghosts and are afraid to admit it. I was going to have to side with the believers. How could I not believe when it happened right before my very eyes?

As I continued doing my research on the computer, I came across manifestation and how there were different stages. Isn't that what Jaxon had said he was doing ... manifesting? I read a lot of articles on manifesting, which left me on with more questions. How could a researcher determine the stages of manifestation? They couldn't experience it themselves. It's not like they died and came back to tell the tale. I shook my head and chuckled as I thought about a journalist interviewing a ghost. I pictured the interviewer with a microphone in his hand pushing it into the face of a ghost asking, "How does it feel to be dead?" *Too funny.* It struck me that I had to stop with the sarcasm about these writers; after all, wasn't I just talking to a ghost myself? Giving the writers of these articles I researched the benefit of the doubt, I continued to read.

The articles did have a lot of facts that were relatable to my experience. I read how there were many types of occurrences when dealing with manifestations. It could be a scent or a smell that you may recognize, or the tactile stage which is being touched or tugged. Temperature changes were another form, apparently ghosts need to use heat for energy or use the energy from other living things around them. Sound is another method of manifestation; footsteps, the sound of something moving, music or speech. And of course, the biggie, visual manifestation. Appearing in physical form; from a cloudlike form to a normal looking living person! Seriously?! I could not believe what I was reading, I had experienced almost every single one of these stages.

I decided to stop the research and lay down for a moment. My head was starting to hurt, and I felt exhausted as it had been such an emotional day. I closed my eyes to rest and immediately fell into a deep sleep. My dream was dark till a swirling scene of clouds appeared and wispy figures started to emerge. I looked right and left trying to determine who the figures were. I reached out to see if I could feel anything, but it was nothing but misty air. My eyes roamed the scene trying to find something recognizable. It was then that I saw a figure in the distance. Wait, was that Jaxon? I could tell by the way he stood there, looking like he had just come from working in the fields. He looked all hot, sweaty, and tanned from the sun. Jaxon looked up and recognized that I was there and smiled, giving me that famous mischievous smile with his dimples shining in all their glory. Oh, that damn face. He was so handsome, and I had developed a serious crush on him.

He stretched his hand out to me as if he wanted me to come closer. There was no question if I would follow him anywhere, I knew I would. My schoolgirl infatuation had made me weak, and I readily accepted his invitation. I started walking towards him and he looked pleased that I was trusting him. I ached for him. I had never felt like this over someone and knew I could not be with him, he was gone ... dead.

As I was walking towards him, I could see the pleasure in his eyes that I was coming to him. Quickly, he looked behind himself, as if he could hear something. What was he looking for? It seemed he was further away than I thought, so I kept on walking trying to reach him. I did not see anything other than Jaxon; he took my total attention. Suddenly he looked behind him again and threw up his hands as if to tell me to stop. I thought he was trying to tell me something. I saw him mouth something, but I could not hear him. I only saw the fear appear in his eyes.

A dark thick mist came from behind Jaxon and began to surround him. I yelled for him to wait for me, but he shook his head vigorously as if to tell me not to come. I watched in terror as I saw his eyes grow wide and with what may have been a silent scream, he was sucked backwards into the mist.

I stood still trying to figure out what I had just witnessed. In Jaxon's absence, the dark mist started to swirl again. I watched as it moved faster until I was almost dizzy. While the darkness started to surround me, I could see what looked like faces coming in and out of my vision. Turning to run in the opposite direction, I found I could not move my feet. My legs were stiffened as I was kept frozen in place. It felt like I had no control over my body. Something was keeping me here on purpose.

Feeling something, I looked down at my feet. A thick black liquid substance had oozed its way towards me, slowly lapping up against my feet and ankles. I wanted to move and get out of this place but couldn't lift my legs. Watching in fear, the waves of this black liquid swelled like a river around me. I was afraid that this sludge would eventually drown me. Again, I tried kicking my feet to run, anything I could do to get out of this blackness, but they would not budge. The black river had swelled to my hips, getting deeper and deeper. I was worried that this could be my death. In a panic, I began looking for something, anything that I could possibly grab onto to pull myself out of this danger. But there was nothing and I didn't know how I was going to get out of here.

The faces in the mist were surrounding me. Running in and out of my vision. They kept coming closer and closer. "Get away from me!" I shrieked. Using my hands, I tried shooing them away. My fear was palatable at this point, my throat was tight, and my tongue felt thick; I could barely swallow. A face came in close to mine. It was grotesquely marred with its skin ripped in what looked like shreds of flesh falling from its face. I screamed at the top of my lungs, and it laughed at me, turning to go back into the vapor. I could see and hear others as they were yelling out, crying, or laughing haughtily at me. I wanted to scream; I wanted to cry. The horror I felt at this moment was indescribable.

What is this hellish place?! I could not seem to get out of this dream. I looked up and saw a bright light appear in the middle of all the dark mist. Could this finally be the end? The black muck was over my waist at this point, and I was too tired to fight this blackness much more. My emotions were on edge, and I thought I would soon drown.

Without warning I could no longer feel any emotion. I became numb, frozen like a statue. As the thick black sludge continued to rise, my fear no longer consumed me. I knew this would be my death. I could not survive this. Hadn't I always heard if you die in your dreams, you will surely die in life? I did not know how true that was, but it seemed I was going to find out.

Out of the bright light within the deep dark haze, appeared a large monstrous form that sauntered forward in a floating wave. I could not make out its features. The only thing I could see, was the outline of it. It floated towards me as if there were nothing to hinder its pace. Everything ceased to exist. The place had taken on a silence, an emptiness of death, and I knew this figure was the cause.

The sludge was up to my shoulders at this stage, making it harder to breathe. I wanted to give up and drown in the sludge but found myself gripped at this figure coming towards me. It stopped about three feet in front of me as if I were a disease, not wanting to get to close to me. As if I repelled it. Ha! The feeling was mutual! It raised up a hand, palm forward, and the thick black liquid stopped. Thank God! I guess I was not going to die from drowning, at least not yet.

After a few moments of studying me, the black form, able to float through the sludge without struggle, came closer towards me. It was humungous, filling up the space in front of me, making sure it was all I could see. I closed my eyes so I would not look into this monster's eyes as it leaned down and put its face in front of mine. I could feel it examining me. I felt the iciness as it surrounded my shoulders and head, as if it were touching my soul.

I kept my eyes shut tight, sensing the monster had gotten right up in my face. Suddenly, I felt nothing. I was hollow, as if this thing had sucked all the feelings right out of me. Surely this was the end for me. Then, without warning it hissed at me in a deep gnarly sneer, "Stay … away" and with a penetrating sound, it raged through me. At long last, I finally found my voice and screamed out loud.

I woke up in a panic! Patting every part of my body, I wanted to make sure I was whole. The hideous creature had seared itself in my memory as it had surged through my being! I guess I screamed out loudly because my aunt was running up the stairs.

Shaking me she cried out, "Alisa! Alisa what happened? Are you all right?"

Dazed, I answered. "Yeah ... I'm not sure what happened, I guess I had a bad dream," I said still panting as I pulled myself up in a sitting position, hugging my knees to my chest.

"Oh sweetheart," Aunt Val came to my bed side and pulled me over into her arms. "Do you want to tell me about it? Do you even remember what it was about?"

Oh, I remembered all right, and there was no way in hell I was going to tell her how I thought I was going to die with all those monsters I had seen. I would not even know where to begin to explain what I had witnessed.

"No, Aunt Val, I can't remember that much of it. I was in darkness and thought I saw something. I don't know, something scared me, that's all."

"Well, we all have those wild and crazy dreams sometimes. I do hope you don't have any more like that, you must have been scared. I have never heard you scream like that before!" Aunt Val hugged me again. "I would say to get some rest, but I don't think you're going to want to go back to sleep for a while," she chuckled.

I did feel better with Aunt Valerie next to me. I held onto her tightly, almost not wanting her to leave, but I wanted to be alone with my thoughts. "Thanks, Aunt Val. I'll be down in a little while."

"Good, because dinner is just about ready. And there is nothing better to help you forget bad dreams than my awesome cooking skills!"

I laughed out loud in agreement on that truism. Aunt Valerie was the best cook I knew!

Chapter 12

That night I decided I really needed to talk to Nikki. We talked almost every day, sometimes briefly, other times an hour or more. Tonight, was going to be one of those long conversation nights! I gave her a call and we made it through all the small talk. We talked about our day and what had been going on. She was telling me about one of our friends caught in a most embarrassing moment. I was amused but did not laugh, as she was. That was her trigger ... she knew me so well.

"Ok, spill." She demanded.

"I don't know what you are talking about!" I tried to sound nonchalant.

"I tell you about the most embarrassing thing that happened to Kara, and you don't even laugh? I know there is something definitely going on. You better start talking, girl, or I'm going to call your Aunt Valerie!"

"No you won't!" I shouted out. Not meaning it to sound so harsh, I took a calming breath, readjusted the sound of my voice and continued. "You don't have to do anything so drastic as that. I just have so much to talk to you about that I'm trying to decide where to start. But please, don't think I'm crazy when I tell you my story. I know it's going to sound unbelievable."

"You know I'll believe whatever you tell me, Alisa, especially if *you* say it's true. I don't think you've ever lied to me before. I won't judge or make fun of you. As your best friend, you should know me better than that."

"I do, so I'll tell you. But you have to promise me that you won't repeat a word of it!"

"Scout's honor … I promise," she replied. I chuckled as I pictured her sitting there with her three fingers up, giving the honor of secrecy.

"Okay, here it goes. I think I encountered a ghost." There I said it. It sounded just as ridiculous out loud as it did in my head.

There was silence on the other end of the line. Finally, Nikki cleared her voice and spoke. "Why do you think that, Alisa? What did you see?"

"I was over at Grace's house. You know, the family I told you about that lives across the road from us?"

"Sure, I remember."

"Well, I decided to go into the barn and pet the horses. When I went in there, I saw a person standing there talking to Grey, my favorite horse. When I really took a moment and looked at him, it was Jaxon. Grace's son that died."

"Oh! The guy you keep talking about in the picture?" She asked.

"Yes, and …" I stopped. The next line was going to make me sound insane. I wasn't sure I could believe it, let alone, tell another person about it. It was crazy to think it really happened.

"Keep going Alisa, you have to tell me now. I'll go nuts if I don't hear the rest of the story." She laughed, which made it easier for me to continue.

I took a deep breath and let it fly as I spoke. "He talked to me, Nikki. Like, we had a real conversation! Am I crazy? Could it all be in my head?"

"What do *you* think?" She asked calmly. I was so glad she was down-to-earth rational. I, on the other hand, was going off the rails. I needed her to reel me back in from crazy town as I explained the rest of my experience.

"It was so real! He told me things about himself that I had not learned from Grace, so it must be real. Then, and this is the wildest part of my story... He let me touch him and he in turn touched me. Our hands that is, we were curious. Plus, I wanted to feel what his being was like."

"Uh huh, of course, you wanted to feel him," Nikki teased accusingly.

"It was just his hand and ... don't you roll your eyes at me, Nikki Carino." It was then I was finally able to laugh for the first time since my dream this afternoon. "I know sarcasm when I hear it."

"Well, I see what you mean. It does sound a little out there. I mean, you touched each other. He spoke? I thought ghosts were just spirits running around and making things go bump in the night. How were you able to see him?"

"Exactly my same thought! I guess I'm attuned to spirits or something, at least that's what Jaxon is guessing."

"Ooohhh, like an Empath? I've heard of those before."

"What's an Empath?"

"You know, where you can feel what others are feeling and see things that others may not be able to see because of an openness you have. Which makes sense, I've seen you get depressed when I am down. And when I am happy, you tend to get cheery too."

"That's nothing unique. I think everyone is like that, feeling what others feel."

"No, you're thinking sympathy and encouragement. I am talking genuine sadness and real elation along with other actual emotions I've seen from you. I don't know why I never recognized it before."

"How do you know so much about this stuff? It's not like we learned it in school or anything."

"You may not have learned it, but I took that Psych class last year, remember? We learned all about the different types of traits of a human being. Empathy was the one trait we debated in class. Is it a trait or a skill? I still say it's a trait. Being an Empath though, takes the trait one step further and gives you an openness that others do not have. I really wish you would have been in that class with me, it was so interesting and fun!"

"Well then maybe you can help me figure out the dream I had today, Dr. Carino. I swear on my life, it was the craziest thing I have ever experienced!"

I proceeded to tell her about the dream and how it literally took the breath right out of me in a panic. I was still feeling the aftereffects even these many hours later. I told her about how it had started with Jaxon, and then his disappearance. I described the faces I had seen, and the thick black sludge that held me captive, making us wonder what it could have represented. We talked about the fact that I was unable to speak, and that the emptiness of my emotions felt like death to me. Finally, I told her about the dark looming figure that warned me to stay away.

After several hours of discussion and trying to figure out what everything could mean, we were still pretty much at ground zero. It was a warning, and Jaxon had been a part of it, that was for sure. Did it mean stay away from Jaxon? But why? He is a ghost, not a human being. It was only a dream anyway. Nikki thought maybe the dream was brought on by doing so much research about ghosts on the internet. Maybe seeing all the different scary pictures on my computer got into my subconscious. Combine that with my visit from Jaxon and having that on my mind. It was probably a typical nightmare, Nikki said, and she was probably right.

I felt so much better after talking it out with Nikki. I promised her that I would see when she could come to Cedar Mills for a visit. I needed to see her soon. I was missing her as much as I missed my mom. We said our goodbyes and I sighed. It was getting late, and I would have to go to bed soon. I decided that I would fill my mind with something other than all this nightmarish stuff we had been talking about. I grabbed the book off the nightstand I had been reading for my summer reading assignments. At least this had love and heroism in it, not demons. It was everything I enjoyed reading. Reading until pure exhaustion took me and I fell into a deep and dreamless sleep.

Chapter 13

The next day Grace called to see if I was available to babysit Elsie. They had an unexpected meeting with the farming counsel and could not take her with them. Of course, I agreed and quickly got myself ready. I was about to walk across the road to Grace's house when something yellow caught my eye at the foot of our mailbox. I looked down to inspect what it could be and noticed a sunflower laying there. I reached down and picked it up, holding it to my nose. I couldn't help but smell it. The scent was fresh, and I could tell it was newly cut. So odd though, I don't remember seeing any sunflowers in the house for Aunt Valerie nor does she grow them. I thought someone must have lost it or tossed it by accident. I don't know how the flower got there. However it landed there, it was beautiful, and I wanted to keep it.

I quickly went back into the house and asked Aunt Valerie to put it in a glass of water for me. She looked at me with confusion in her eyes, so I had to tell her how I had found the flower. I was in a hurry, not wanting to be late. I said my goodbye for the second time and ran back out of the house.

Crossing the road, I rushed down the driveway, making it just in time for Grace and Charles to leave. Charles looked like he was in a mood, not one to be reckoned with. I had a feeling he and Grace had been arguing before I arrived. Grace, however, gave me her ever-loving smile and instructions. Lunch was in the refrigerator, and they should be home in time for dinner. If not, she had leftovers ready for us. I knew the routine by now, but I let her go on. We said our goodbyes and they left.

Elsie came roaring down the stairs with two dolls in her hands. As I saw her running towards me, I knelt on one knee, and she lunged herself into me, hugging me. I laughed and held her tight for a moment.

"Can we play dollies today? I have my room all set up and then we can have a tea party afterwards."

"Whoa, slow down, short stuff! I just got here." I said as I was trying to get back into a standing position. "I think we should play dollies until lunch time, then we will take a walk before tea party time. How does that sound?"

"I like it! I'm ready ... come on!"

She was so full of enthusiasm, and it was contagious. I followed her upstairs and sure enough, she had everything all set up. We played house with the dolls and made little stuffed animals our pets. We were having fun playing when Elsie suddenly blurted out "My parents fight sometimes."

Hold on, where did this come from? I didn't know why she was telling me this. So, I took a pause, thinking maybe she had been holding this in for a while. Maybe she needed to get it out and tell someone she could trust. If she trusted me enough to talk about something personal, I would give her my full attention. I put my doll down and slowly took the one she was holding and set it down next to mine.

"Everyone fights with the people they love from time-to-time Elsie." I spoke gently to her.

"But it makes me feel sad." She pouted.

"It's okay to feel sad; just know it is not your fault that they argue."

"They always fight, and it gets bad sometimes. Daddy gets mean."

I was afraid to ask the next question, but I had to know. Elsie was confiding in me, and I wanted to make sure she was alright. "Has ... has he hit any of you?"

"No," she shook her head. "He hits walls or breaks stuff. But he always says he's sorry afterwards." She looked up at me with hope in her eyes. As if to ask if that was acceptable. I was so thankful to know he didn't hurt them. I wasn't sure how I would've reacted if I found out someone was beating on Grace and Elsie.

"Well, I *am* glad to hear that he doesn't hit you, but he should not break things either Elsie." I didn't want to get too involved and say something that Grace would disapprove of. Nor did I know what she would say if she knew Elsie was telling me personal information.

"Daddy and Jaxon used to fight a lot too," she said looking down at the floor. I could tell this made her sad to talk about as well.

"I'm sorry to hear that," I said gently putting my hand on her arm encouraging her to continue. "What did they fight about?"

"Daddy would always be mean to Jaxon. He made him work hard. Even when he'd just finished chores and was tired. They got into it all the time and it would get really bad. I sometimes thought they were going to hit each other! It always made me scared when they did that." Elsie shuddered and shook her head as if the memory were too much to think about. But she continued on, lowering her voice to a near whisper. "I know the real reason Daddy was mean to Jaxon."

"Why is that?" I asked, wanting her to continue.

"Jaxon said it was because he always stuck up for Momma. Every time Daddy would start yelling at Momma, Jaxon didn't want her to fight him alone. He said Momma didn't like him fighting for her, but Jaxon wouldn't stop! He did it anyway and I was happy about that. Now that Jaxon is gone, she doesn't have anyone to fight for her. I can't do it, I'm afraid to make Daddy mad."

Oh hell, that was a lot for one little kid to carry. I wanted her to know that I was here for her. "Elsie, I want you to know I am proud of you for talking to me."

"Really?!" She beamed that beautiful face at me. I guess this encouraged her because she decided to go on.

"I miss Jaxon so much. He was the bestest brother ever. He played with me all the time."

"I heard. Your Mommy told me all about that." I grinned at her, knowing the stories Grace had already told me about the two of them.

She smiled as if she were living in the memories at that moment. "When Momma and Daddy would fight, I would hear them and start crying. Jaxon would come to my room to see if I was okay. I'd always ask him to lay next to me so I could stop crying. He would pat my back and give me a hug saying everything was okay and that helped me feel better."

"That sounds like a very nice big brother you had. He loved you so much!"

"Yeah, he did," she gently laughed, then continued, "He always did this thing before he left me. He'd always say he loved me and then drew on my forehead with his finger an X and then circle it." She mimicked the same motions on my forehead. "He used to do that to me all the time, even when I wasn't scared or crying."

"Why did he do that?" I said curiously.

She gave me a big grin. "He said he wanted to leave me with his hugs and kisses on my mind."

Oh my God, I loved it! That was so sweet of him to do that for her. He left her with a beautiful memory, something she will have to hold on to forever. Elsie stopped smiling suddenly and started to cry.

"Alisa ... I really miss my brother so much. I want him to be here with me." She said in between her sniffles.

"He is here, Elsie. Right here." I said pointing to her heart. "He is always there in your heart. Think about all the love you two shared. He loved you so much and I know you love him." Then I pointed to her head. "He is also here in your mind with all your memories. And I know he is still thinking of you and looking out for you even though he is no longer physically here. Do you understand what I mean?" I wished I could tell her the real truth, that he *was* here all the time watching out for her.

"I think I understand." Then she lowered her voice in secret. "Sometimes when I really miss him bad, I sneak into his room and sit on his bed. I even grab his pillow or something he used to wear and try to smell him. But I can't seem to smell him anymore."

"That's okay Elsie, just because you can't smell him doesn't mean you have forgotten him. Can you remember that for me?" I waited until she shook her head yes before continuing. "At least you have lots of good memories with Jaxon. Better memories than most people have with their brothers that are still living."

"That's true." She took her finger and started jabbing it into my arm. "I love you, Alisa!"

"I love you too, shortcake! Now are you getting hungry? It's lunchtime and I am on empty!"

"Yes!" She jumped up and we both ran our way down to the kitchen.

Chapter 14

"Alisa, can you please come here?" I heard Aunt Valerie call for me.

"Just a moment!" I jumped up and ran down the stairs to see what she needed.

"I need to go into town today and thought you would like to go with me. Maybe we could get you some clothes for school and a new pair of shoes."

I internally rolled my eyes. I hated shopping for clothes, trying everything on was such a chore. Shoes, no problem! I could stand to get another pair of running shoes, which I love. "Sure, Aunt Val. Sounds like fun." I lied. I was however, a little excited about going to town to get my favorite latte. I hadn't had one in a while and the thought really cheered me up.

We readied ourselves and headed out the door. As we drove to the end of the driveway, I noticed another sunflower was haphazardly sitting at the base of the mailbox. Just like the day before! "Aunt Val, stop for a moment." I got out of the car and picked up the flower.

"You found one of those yesterday; it can't be a coincidence." Aunt Val looked at me inquisitively. "Do you want me to go back to the house so you can put it in the same vase as the other one?"

I didn't want to be a bother since we were already heading out. But the flower was so beautiful, and I did not want it to die while in a hot car. "Would you mind? I mean I know we were on our way out. I don't want to be an inconvenience."

"Nonsense! You do know this car has that newfangled thing called reverse, right?"

"Aunt Val," I laughed.

Aunt Valerie backed her way to the house so I could quickly run the flower into the house and add it to the vase. It was really pretty to see both flowers sitting in the vase and it brought a smile to my lips. I started thinking about what Aunt Val had said, that this was not a coincidence. Someone was leaving these here for me to find. I hoped they were for me, or maybe Aunt Val had a secret admirer. I snickered at the thought, I would have to tease her about this.

If the flowers were for me, I tried to consider who could be leaving them. My smile began to fade as I hoped to God it wasn't Grayson. I knew he drove past our house from time to time, especially when he was racing. He could have easily thrown a flower out of the window of his car as he drove by. But that seemed like something beneath him. Not showy enough. He would want to make sure that I knew he gave me these flowers.

Roger? That thought also made me shudder. I wanted no part of that. However, I didn't think that he was the thoughtful type. I wasn't sure he would even think about girls liking flowers. The idea of Roger trying to woo a girl seemed unlikely.

As we drove into town I could not stop obsessing over where the flowers were coming from. I decided to tease my aunt. "Aunt Val, do you have a secret admirer?"

She looked shocked with complete surprise that I would even ask such a thing. "Absolutely not! Why do you ask?"

"I don't know … I am just trying to figure out why you keep getting these flowers. Who is bringing them? I had assumed they were for me, but then the thought occurred, they may be for you."

"Alisa Renee Christi! You should know better than that." Aunt Valerie laughed out loud. "Besides, I'm already taken. And if Uncle Henry brought me flowers, he sure as hell would not leave them at the mailbox. He knows I'd knock him upside the head for that!" She popped herself in the head for example. "Besides, I truly believe they are for my beautiful niece."

"Thanks, but I can't figure who would give them to me. And one at a time is just weird." We talked the rest of the way to town. The flowers were forgotten while we enjoyed the rest of the day shopping together.

Aunt Val was in a shopping frenzy, and I was completely exhausted! By the time we were done, I had five new outfits for school and two pairs of shoes. I would have to let my mom know about these purchases when I talked to her tonight. I'm sure she wouldn't mind that I bought some things for school, but I was feeling a little guilty. *I'll just blame it on Aunt Val,* I thought, laughing to myself.

I ran to get a cup of coffee while Aunt Val was still in the shoe store. I bought us a couple of lattes and ran out the door. As I was leaving, I ran right into Grayson and almost spilled the coffees on myself. "Oh my God! You almost made me burn myself!" I scorned him. Was he waiting for me or was this just another coincidence?

"Thank goodness you are okay," he said looking me up and down. "How are you, my sweet flower? I haven't seen you around lately." He gave me that gorgeous smile of his that made me sick. I knew he was turning on what he thought was charm. Yuck! He knows how I feel about him. "You know what they say ... absence makes the heart grow fonder."

"Seriously?! I'm not fond of you at all, and your absence definitely makes my life better!" I said clinching my teeth. He really got under my skin. First, he was horrible to me when we first met, and now he thinks he can charm me into good graciousness? I thought he didn't like me, *not his type*, he said. *That* was one thing I was not going to forget! I would have to remind him of this fact as he stood there trying to be sugary-sweet towards me.

He laughed out loud and caressed my cheek with his thumb. "You really are something. I do appreciate good humor in my women."

The look I gave him made him laugh that much harder as he walked off. I was fuming mad at this point. Thank goodness Aunt Valerie was coming to pick me up with the car. I gave her the latte I'd purchased for her and got into the car blowing out a long breath.

"I'm tired too!" She said, mistaking my whoosh of breath for being tired.

"I'm not tired, just angry and trying to calm down." I fumed.

"Why? What happened at the coffee shop?"

"Nothing happened *in* the coffee shop; it's what happened *outside* of the coffee shop. I ran into our favorite person ... Grayson. Ooh, he really gets under my skin. So conceited! He just thinks he's God's gift to all women. Well, not this woman!" I spewed out.

Aunt Valerie laughed and said, "Thank the Lord!" as she sped off towards home.

Later that night, after talking to my mom, I called Nikki. I was telling her about Grayson and how he assumed I would just fall all over him. This drew her curiosity. I had mentioned Grayson before, but now he was really getting under my skin. First, she asked me what he looked like again, which I did in all his glorious detail. I don't know if she was asking me to describe him for my benefit or for herself! I had to admit, he really was something to look at, which did not appease me at all.

"He sounds so delicious!" Nikki giggled.

"Please, do not heart throb over him. He is nothing but a big pain in the ass!" I complained.

"Yeah, but you know you like the attention he's giving you. Kind of like the forbidden fruit. You know you want some but know you shouldn't." And this time she laughed ... hard! She knew she was right, and I hated that. I wasn't about to give in to him, though. I'd never give him the satisfaction of winning me over. I said as much to Nikki, but she wouldn't hear of it. She accused me of playing the hard-to-get role.

I wasn't playing hard-to-get. I truly did not like this guy and told her so. She started snickering again and saying I was in denial. Telling me I needed to come clean. As if! Besides, I was secretly crushing on Jaxon and we both knew it, but I wasn't going to talk about that tonight. We chatted a while longer and then said our goodbyes. I was going to have to get her here so she could see what I was talking about. She really needed to see what a jerk Grayson truly was. I just hope he wasn't the one giving me the flowers. But he did call me a flower today ... and I thought about that until I drifted off to sleep.

That night I dreamt about Grayson. I dreamt that he handed me a bouquet of sunflowers and I accepted them readily, smiling up at him. We walked leisurely along a path in a parting of flowering trees. Taking my hand, he led me toward a beautiful pond.

It was a beautiful summer day. The sun was glistening off the water and I could see small ripples lapping the shoreline. A blanket had been laid out in the grass near the pond with a basket next to it. He took my flowers and laid them beside the basket. He took my hand and brought me down to sit on the blanket next to him. He then opened the basket and surprised me with some strawberries, grapes, bread, cheese, and a pitcher of iced tea.

I felt so special, as I lifted my face up to the sun catching the warmth from the rays. Basking in the glow of the sun I couldn't help glancing over at Grayson's handsome face. The sun played with the highlights in his hair and his blue eyes shone bright. He was magnificent to look at.

We talked and laughed while we ate the picnic lunch he had brought, truly enjoying each other's company. The enjoyment of Grayson was something new to me. I had grown to accept the loathing and disgust he usually made me feel when he opened his mouth.

Taking a strawberry, Grayson held it to my mouth, wanting me to take a bite. I paused. I was not about to get romantic with him, he made me sick! It was then he took the opportunity to look at me with his smoldering eyes and … damn it! I was a goner. I took the bite and swallowed as he rubbed the rest of the strawberry on my lips. Coming closer towards me, he leaned in and kissed me. I don't know why, but I couldn't find the strength to stop him. Maybe it was the taste of the strawberry on our lips, but I gave into the moment and felt the wonder of his lips touching mine.

Warmth filled me all over and he pulled me closer to him, sinking his mouth into mine for a deeper kiss. His hand wandered, gently caressing my face then down my neck to the crevice of my breasts.

I could not stop his hands nor his unbroken kiss. His lips felt warm and soft as they worked their magic on me and his hands were like fire on my skin. I could tell he was very skilled, and the thought gave me momentary pause. I did not want to be another notch on his belt, but in this moment, I could not seem to stop myself. He was enticing my mouth, and my body was following suit.

Slowly he laid me down and lay himself next to me, rekindling the desire with his kisses. His hands began to wander all over my body, and I felt engulfed with every touch. I slid my arms around his neck and pulled him in to me, crushing him even closer to my body. I had never felt like this before. Grayson finally broke the kiss, knowing I didn't want it to end. I was putty in his hands. He held me captive, looking into my eyes as he spoke to me. "I told you I could have you if I wanted to." I screamed furiously and woke up!

I must have woken the whole house up because I heard my Aunt Valerie and Uncle Henry running to my room. "Alisa, what's wrong? What's going on?" My Aunt Val asked.

"I'm sorry, I must have had another bad dream. I don't know why they keep happening! I've never had these many nightmares before."

Uncle Henry came forward and sat down next to me while Aunt Valerie stood in the doorway. "Maybe you're just missing your old life while you are trying to adjust to living here. Your subconscious could be upset!" Uncle Henry said. I loved Uncle H, but this was not the issue. This was a girl thing, and I am sure Aunt Val would understand. If I wanted to talk to her about it, which right now, I didn't.

"You're probably right, Uncle Henry." I lied. "I'll try and get back to sleep. Sorry I woke you two up." Uncle Henry beamed as if he had just solved the world's problems, and I smiled back as he gave me a bear hug.

I knew Aunt Valerie was not buying it and she looked directly into my eyes. "Whenever you are really ready to talk, I will be waiting." She walked towards me and gave me a kiss on my forehead, saying goodnight. I wanted to talk to her, but who knew where to start? Would she even believe me or think I was going mad? Whatever I did, I would have to find a way to stop these damned dreams!

Chapter 15

It had been a busy past couple of days which meant I was not able to get over to Grace's house for a visit. I decided today would be a good day to walk on over and see Grey the horse. And if Grace were not busy, I could check in on her as well. I still felt a little uneasy knowing about their problems Elsie had told me in confidence, but I would never use that as an excuse to not visit. Besides, secretly I was hoping Jaxon would show himself to me again.

As I left the house to go across the road, plain as day, was another sunflower lying at the foot of the mailbox. Like someone had just tossed it there. I smiled as I picked it up and carried it with me as I walked to Grace's house. I looked straight at the house while I walked the long driveway. There it stood in all its glory, and I could feel a connection to it. Was it strange to feel so drawn to a house as if it were calling out to me?

I glanced to the right and saw the old fenced-in cemetery under the oak tree. Jaxon's body lay there while his spirit was roaming the farm. My mind couldn't wrap itself around that. I had never known death before coming here. I was too young to remember my father's death, and my grandparents had already passed before I was born. I looked down at the ground as I was walking before looking back at the house, trying to dismiss the thoughts of death in my mind.

My imagination must have taken on a mind of its own. As I looked around the yard of the house, I could see people from the 1800's dressed in their Sunday best walking around enjoying a lazy summer afternoon. I could see people playing croquet on the lawn under the large oak tree. Ladies were sitting on the front porch fanning themselves while they enjoyed their tea. On the other side of the yard a picnic table laden with food was sitting under the shade of a tree luring me with the sights of their goods. A woman noticed me and began waving her hand, beckoning me to come over and join them. No! I rubbed my eyes with the palms of my hands. I must be seeing things. Imaginary scenes don't communicate with you.

I shook my head no in response. I decided to ignore her and the others wandering around. The incident had me a little shook up and it was hard to control my nerves. I looked around for Charles' truck but did not see it. Knowing I would be alone I went straight to the barn. The barn was empty as I could not see or feel Jaxon. I was happy to see Grey, walking over to pet this sweet horse for a few minutes. He nuzzled my neck and it made me laugh. I reached up and scratched behind his ear giving him the attention he was seeking.

"Mmmmm, I wish that were me!" I heard a velvet voice say.

Recognizing that voice, I stilled. I quickly turned around to see Jaxon standing there watching me. He made me smile as I took in his handsome face. "I didn't think you were going to show yourself today."

"I would never miss an opportunity, if I have the chance to visit you," he said as he gave me that warm mischievous smile. Damn, I love those dimples! I melt every time he uses them on me.

"And I would never miss an opportunity to *see* you," I said, giving him my best flirtatious smile.

He chuckled and started walking towards the barn door. He turned back to see if I would follow and looked at the flower grasped in my hand. He looked back up into my eyes and said, "Come follow me; I want to show you something."

Without hesitation I swiftly followed him, not knowing how long he had in this form. "Sorry, Grey," I called out, leaving him like a bad habit. The horse bristled at me, and I chuckled. "Where are you taking me?"

"That is going to be a surprise. Let's go!" He said, grabbing my hand.

We started winding around the fences and past the vegetable garden. We turned right and walked down another path in between rows of the soybean crops. Heading towards the back of the property I saw it and stopped in my tracks. "Oh Jaxon, it's amazing!" Then it hit me … the sunflowers … they were from him.

It was a vision! The most beautiful sunflower fields I had ever seen. There must have been acres of these flowers standing tall, row after row. They were magnificent as the sun's rays touched the petals, casting a lovely yellow glow over the fields. I had never seen such a surreal sight; it literally took my breath away. Jaxon was looking at me with smiling eyes and knew he had captured my heart.

"I wanted you to see these, they are my mothers," he said shyly.

"Jaxon, they're beautiful! When did she plant them? There are so many! How did she have the time?" I asked, still in shock from the sight.

"Whoa ... slow down on the questions." He laughed at me. "Actually, my father planted them for her. My real father, Daniel. Not Charles," he said with a frown.

"Your mother told me briefly of him, that he had died while you were a baby."

His eyes looked lost in the past as he began his story. "They were young and in love, that's how she described it to me. Isn't that always the way it begins? My parents got married at a young age and decided to move here to start farming. It was the perfect plan since the house and all the property had been in my mom's family for generations. My father planted the sunflowers first, as a gift to my mom. He wanted to provide her with a bouquet of flowers every now and again. Mom said they were too beautiful, and she stopped him from cutting them down "for no reason" as she put it. She later learned that the seeds were of value if she marketed them. So, she started a small business and was able to use the money to help a little with the bills.

"Then a few years later I showed up. My mother said it was the best time of her life. Her business was growing, the farm was earning money and I was here; everything felt complete. And then my father died in a car crash when I was about fifteen months old, leaving my mom and I alone."

I put her my hand to my chest, I knew what he was feeling. "I'm so sorry, Jaxon, I completely understand. My father died too when I was a baby. It's like you can't remember what it feels like to have them in your life, because you do not have any memories. But there is an empty place in your heart where you know they should be."

"Exactly! That *is* how it feels." He looked at me and ran his hands through his hair as if the next part of his story was a burden to relay. "My mom tried to stay here a while after dad died, but she said the memories were too unbearable. Plus, she couldn't take care of me, run her business, and work a whole farm by herself. So, she locked the place up and moved us back to her parents' house to live, only returning to work the sunflower fields. We stayed with my Grandparents until she married Charles when I was about ten years old. What a disaster that turned out to be!"

"You really don't like Charles, do you?" I asked, searching his face for true feelings.

With a grim expression he replied, "What is there to like? He is arrogant, demanding and downright nasty mean. They argue all the time because he wants to control her and everybody around him. I wanted to get her away from him so badly, but she always refused."

"Maybe she really loves him."

He looked at me with his piercing glare. "How can you love a thorn in your side festering until it bleeds?"

"Wow, that's harsh!" I gasped.

"It's true! He hated me because I would not bend to his will. He also treats everyone around him like total garbage. As if he is God, and we should all bow down and worship him. And if you do not, there is hell to pay," he said irately.

Wanting to bring comfort to his hurt, I made an observation. "Didn't he adopt you when you were younger? There must be some good in him somewhere."

Jaxon threw his head back and laughed out loud. "There is no way in hell he wanted *me!*" he said turning his eyes on me. I was taken aback at the hatred in them. "He only passed off the pretense of *loving me.* He probably thought it would be easier to talk my mother into marrying him if he adopted me. I am especially suspicious of his actions on the day I died."

Hesitating, I asked, "Do you feel comfortable telling me about that day?"

Chapter 16

"It was so damned hot that day!" Describing my last day of life. "Working in the barn, I felt myself slowly melting in the heat. I felt as if there was no escape from heaviness that surrounded me. The air was thick and sweat rolled down my body. The heat was intense everywhere that day, but it was even heavier in the upper part of the barn than down below. *There should be more wind up here* I was thinking to myself, but there was not any wind to be had. It had to be one of the hottest days of summer so far.

"As I was working that day, I noticed all the haybales I had pulled into the loft so far. Standing at the edge of the opening to our two-story pole barn, I peered down to see how many were left to bring up. Pulling on the rigging gear that lifted haybales up into the barn was a very taxing job. One that no one wanted. Which is probably why Charles always made me do it."

Alisa gently grabbed his arm and encouraged him to continue.

"I only had one bale left to go. Pulling in the haybales was quickly wearing me out. The pully system my stepfather had rigged on the outside of the barn did help lift the haybales, but I was still the one that had to pull them up to the top of the barn and haul them in. I looked down again thinking about how high up I was, forty feet - at least! I was glad I did not have to carry the hay up all the ladders. The weight on my shoulders and climbing over and over would have killed me on a day like that.

"I remember Charles calling up to me, "Last bale ready". I reached for the rope to the left side of the doorway. Not wanting the bale to sway, I pulled gently on the rope. Experience taught me that if the bale slid out of its ropes and fell, there would be hell to pay. Charles would blame me for the mess or worse add more chores to my day. I was already exhausted, and my arms were throbbing. But I wouldn't put it past him to up the ante on the chores just to make me suffer that much more. Adding more chores knowing how worn out I was, would just make his day. If there was one thing I knew about Charles, he *loved* to make others suffer. Charles was a stepfather to me and nothing more. A dad? Never a dad."

"I knew he was a little rough around the edges, but I had no idea," Alisa said as she tried to comfort him. She looked at him and said, "Go on".

"I wiped my brow with the back of my hand, but it did nothing to help. It was nothing but sweat wiping sweat. I leaned slightly out of the upper door, and reached out to pull the final hay bale in." I fell silent, trying to recall all the details of my final moments. Alisa waited patiently as he seemed to search for the right words. "Looking back now, I remember noticing a shadow in the corner of the barn. I turned but saw nothing. As I reached out to grab the rope, I felt a hard shove. Stunned, I felt my arms and legs flailing in the empty air. I desperately tried to grab onto the rope, but the rope was out of reach. All I could grab onto was air as the ground came for me. After that, my world went black.

"After I passed, I saw everything unfolding ... which was not easy to watch. I watched Charles as he ran out of the barn to kneel over me, acting concerned when he called for my mother. The devastation of my death threw her into despair. I wasn't sure if she would ever come back from seeing my body lying there motionless, as all life had left me. Obviously, her grief still continues to this very day."

Chapter 17

After hearing Jaxon relay his story, I found myself at a loss. What do you say after that? Only my tears would show my true feelings. He had his own feelings about the whole situation. Who was I to question them? I didn't respond, only letting him speak his mind in hopes he could find some closure. I doubted that closure would be found anytime soon though, with all the animosity he held in regard to Charles. "Maybe we should start heading back, I don't want to lose you while we are all the way out here." I was worried he couldn't stay in his manifested form too much longer and I did not want to be all the way out here alone.

"I'm sorry, I didn't mean to put a damper on the afternoon. I wanted it to be romantic. But I think you may be right. We should probably head back."

My brain froze at romantic, and I stopped in my tracks. He wanted a romantic moment with me. But how ... why? I mean, I couldn't be romantically involved with Jaxon; he wasn't even a physically formed human being. I couldn't deny that there was a strong connection between us. And I would love nothing else but to be with him. However, considering I didn't plan on dying anytime soon and he was *not* going to come back to life, it seemed like a moot point. My mind wrestled with these thoughts as I followed him back to the barn.

Once we got to the barn, I could tell he was leaving me. He seemed tired and his energy was fading. "Jaxon, you should go. You look exhausted."

"I wish I could stay with you longer like this. However, I want you to know … just because I am not physically present, I will always try and be around you while you are here. You will feel me."

"And in my dreams apparently," I chuckled trying to pass it off. He looked at me inquisitively. "Yeah, I dreamt of you the other night. But we can talk about that another time. Go on and unphase or whatever you call it. I will come back, and we can talk soon."

He reached out as he had done before and touched my face, leaving a feeling of iciness on my cheek. "We do need to talk soon; I will be waiting," he said.

"Oh, and Jaxon … thank you for the flowers."

"Anything for you, beautiful." He grinned and faded into nothingness.

Why did he have to leave? The afternoon we had spent together was special and I wanted more time with him. I wished we could have spent the evening together, talking and learning more about each other. After our afternoon together, I felt attached to him; bonded in a way I had never experienced before. Sure, I had dated before, but come to think of it, I don't think I could say I have had a real boyfriend. One that I could feel connected to. Wait … boyfriend?! I had to stop thinking about Jaxon like that. Friend, yes. He is just a friend and nothing more. I would have so much to talk about with Nikki tonight. It was going to be one of those late into the night phone calls I chuckled to myself.

Chapter 18

I did not stop by to see Grace while I was at her house yesterday, so I decided to go and see her today. As usual, there was a sunflower at the base of the mailbox. I ran it back into the house and added it to the other ones. I was going to have to tell Jaxon to stop giving me the sunflowers. Not that I disliked receiving them - I truly did! He made me feel so special knowing he was thinking of me, but I had my reasons to tell him to stop. One big reason was that I didn't want to explain where these flowers were coming from to my aunt. And two, I didn't want Grace to lose any more flowers that she used for her business because of me.

I looked both ways and then crossed the road walking down the long driveway towards the house.

"Beautiful day for a walk, isn't it?"

I jumped and looked to see Jaxon walking along with me. "You scared me!" I said as I swatted his arm. He laughed and then smiled down at me. "Can anybody see you walking with me?"

"No, it seems you are the only one! Makes it a little convenient don't you think?"

"How so?" I asked intrigued by his statement.

"Well, as you know, my family is immune to me. Only the animals and you have the gift of seeing spirits like we discussed the other day. And I am positive there is no one else around here in this town that has such a special gift. Now, I just thought I would come and take a stroll with you."

I laughed at him and his 'taking a stroll'. We slowly walked down the driveway and talked the entire time. If anyone had seen me, I probably would have looked like a nut, talking to myself. I took the opportunity with Jaxon to discuss how I felt about the sunflowers. He wasn't very happy with me about my reasonings at first, but he had to agree. We arrived at the front door, and he kissed my cheek before Grace answered, allowing me to come in. I was taken aback by the kiss and thought it was even crazier to watch Jaxon just waltz through the door with me. Poor Grace had no idea he was even there.

While I visited with Grace, Jaxon went upstairs to see his sister, even though she could not see him physically. He still wanted to be there for her which was, in his mind, what a big brother was supposed to do. I was sure I didn't have to tell him about the story his sister relayed to me. He knew about it all too well; hell, he lived it.

I was getting ready to leave after my visit with Grace, when I saw Jaxon come down the stairs. He waited for his mother to stop talking to me. "So, you will be available to babysit for us tomorrow night? Are you sure it will be okay to stay over?" Grace was asking.

"Of course! I have nothing else going on tomorrow or the next day. Besides, if I need anything, Aunt Valerie and Uncle Henry are right over there." I said pointing across to our house.

"Okay then, I'll see you around 4:30 tomorrow afternoon."

"I will be here!"

Jaxon beamed at me as he proceeded to walk with me out of the house. We stopped by the barn to visit Grey, after which we found a corner to hide in, talking the whole time. We must have been there talking for a few hours when I paused and took a good look at him. I could tell he was getting tired, and I knew it was time for him to go. I insisted he go ahead and leave me, but he refused and walked me back down the driveway towards home.

When we reached the end of the path, Jaxon leaned over and whispered in my ear. "I will be waiting for you, beautiful." I blushed, as he gave me a light kiss on my cheek. God, I was done for! He was so romantic and charming, and I was falling hard, not knowing how to stop it. My mind was beating NO into my brain, while my heart was beating YES.

I shook my head and walked across the road feeling so sad that I had to leave Jaxon. He was still standing there when I turned to look back at him, so I blew him a kiss. He looked so adorable when he grabbed the air for my kiss and pressed it to his heart. It made me melt and want to cry at the same time. He must be so lonely.

"Until tomorrow," he said as he faded away.

"Until tomorrow," I called back to him and went home.

The next day, 4:30 in the afternoon could not come soon enough for me. I was thrilled that I was going to baby sit Elsie, knowing that Jaxon would be there with me. He was at the end of the long drive when I arrived and walked with me to the house talking nonstop. I had to laugh at Jaxon and asked if he had bottled up all his conversation for me.

"Of course I do, about a year's worth. Besides, who else could I talk to? Grey is not much of a conversationalist you know!" He said looking at me with that mischief in his eye. He was in a great mood, and I could tell we were going to have fun today. We were laughing and joking all the way to his house. I had to give him a *knock it off* look when he was mimicking Grace during her final instructions so they could leave. He was cracking up and I was trying desperately not to bust out laughing myself!

Elsie showed up, excited that I was there to babysit, and I knew my night would be filled with activity. Sure enough, she had the whole evening planned out! We played and visited the horses, ate dinner, and played some more. When it was time to take a bath, she put up a small fight, but I was able to talk her into the bath by promising dessert and a movie afterwards. She had me suckered and she knew it. I chuckled because really... who cared? Of course, I wouldn't let her know that I was on to her. Besides, she was so damned cute!

Throughout the evening I could feel Jaxon everywhere. Whether it was a whisp of cold air passing by me or a tug on my ponytail, his presence made me smile. At one point during the night, Elsie asked me what I was smiling about. I told her it was because she was so beautiful it put a smile on my lips. It was not a complete lie; she truly was beautiful, and I enjoyed our time together. I sure as hell was not going to say I was smiling about her brother!

Elsie and I sat together on the couch to watch a movie before she had to go to bed. She was sitting on my left and I could feel Jaxon's presence on my right. It felt right to have him next to me, almost as if we were on a date. I felt his cool touches on my arm, my face, and the back of my neck. When he gently blew into my ear, it made me shiver. Elsie looked at me inquisitively, "Just a chill," I explained. She seemed satisfied with that answer and continued to watch the movie. I turned my face towards where I knew Jaxon was and gave him an evil eye, and without seeing it, I could tell he was chuckling at me.

Halfway through the movie Elsie fell asleep. I picked her up and took her to her bed, tucking her in. She gave me a sleepy half smile and rolled over, falling back into a heavy sleep. I shut the door to her room and felt Jaxon's presence in the hall. "Come with me," he whispered. I quietly followed him to his room, gently shutting the door behind me and turned on the light. I turned back around and saw Jaxon had manifested himself so I could see him.

"You are getting good at this; have you been practicing?" I asked.

"Let's just say I have been inspired lately." I felt my cheeks turn hot, and hoped I was not blushing as hard as it felt. "Would you like to listen to some music?" He asked as he motioned for me to sit on the bed.

I didn't know why, but I was nervous. "Yeah, sure, I like some of that classic rock you have. Just keep it low so we don't wake up Elsie. That would be very awkward if she found me in here."

He chuckled and put on some music then turned back to look at me trying to make me feel at ease. "Relax, I'm just wanting to hang out with you, listen to some tunes and talk some. I'm not going to attack you."

"Are you *sure* that is all you want?" I said in the most alluring voice I could muster teasing him.

"Don't tempt me," he said seductively looking me in the eyes. He slowly walked over and sat down next to me. Taking my hand into his, he began to gently rub the back of it. Knowing that it was probably too cold for me, he released it and we both fell silent.

"Do you want to talk about that dream you had with me in it?" he asked.

"No ... not right now. I don't want to ruin this time I have with you talking about bad dreams. We can discuss it tomorrow if you walk me home."

"It would be my honor to walk you home," he beamed at me.

I was jittery sitting beside him as we both searched for something to say. For as much conversation as we had made the past couple of days, we were having trouble finding something to talk about. He lifted his head and locked his eyes into mine moving in closer to me. My hands were trembling, and I felt a shiver run down my spine.

"Are you cold?" he asked.

"No," I whispered, "you make me ... nervous."

Jaxon grinned and took my face in his hands lifting it up to meet his. He leaned in and gave me a gentle kiss. The kiss was cool, soft, and tender. He paused, as if he were asking for permission to kiss me again. I gently nodded my head saying it was alright. I sat still as he brought me close and kissed me again this time with more passion. It was intense and full of emotion. The temperature of his body was a sharp contrast to the heat he generated in me.

Relishing his lips on mine, I knew I didn't want this to end. The music playing in the background gave ambiance to the room. I was swirled by the sounds, relaxed in the resonance of it. Jaxon leaned back and pulled my ponytail out of its holder, and I felt my hair falling around my shoulders.

His eyes widened and he looked surprised. Reaching out he touched a curl. "Your hair is magnificent. Like a mane of waves flowing down around you."

"Thank you." I blushed, looking down folding my hands together in my lap. He made me feel so beautiful, but I was not used to the compliments.

The room was thickening with anticipation between us, and I wanted him to touch me again, kiss me again. He ran his hands through my hair feeling each strand as they fell through his fingers. I trembled with anxiousness, the butterflies whirling in my stomach when I heard the music stop. Caught up in our moment, the silence became loud when we found nothing to say to each other.

He got up and quickly looked through his music, deciding on a CD. I took that opportunity to move up further on the bed. I curled up on my side, getting comfortable. I was tired from my day's activities with Elsie and closed my eyes for a second. He walked back over towards the bed and saw me lying there. I was so close to sleep when I heard him chuckle and ask, "Are you comfortable on *my* bed?"

"Mmmhmm," I mumbled.

I felt him sit back down on the bed and reach over to rub my arm up and down. "I truly wish I had met you when I was living. It doesn't seem fair to meet someone like you in my afterlife. Not fair at all!"

"Sshh, don't think about that right now. I know you're not going to be able to stay like this for long."

I knew he could not stay in his manifested form, and I would be losing him soon. I reached over and pulled him down next to me. I heard him blow out a breath in order to keep himself in control. We talked for a while longer, describing our perfect dream dates. I rolled onto my back to look at the ceiling, thinking how sad it was that we would never know those moments together. He took that instant to hold my hand and we continued to listen to the music quietly. When the CD was done, he got back up and changed it for a new one.

When he came back to his bed and lay back down beside me, my stomach was so full of nerves. Why did he make me so anxious? Jaxon rolled over onto his side to face me, and we talked a few more minutes while he played with my hair. Finally, he turned my head to face his. "I have to kiss you again," he said with his eyes smoldering into mine. I fell silent and again shook my head in approval.

The kiss was cold and sweet. He hesitated, then kissed the corner of my mouth, my lips and my cheek, pausing again. Looking in my eyes, he questioned me again without speaking, wanting to know if he should continue. His uncertainty and wavering was a charming quality as he waited for my reaction. My response was immediate ... I wanted more. The chill of his lips lost their iciness to me when he furthered his kiss and took my mouth with passion. I was heated through as I put my arms around his neck when he leaned over to kiss me intensely. I had never felt like this before. It was better than any dream I had ever had.

I pulled him closer to me in a crushing embrace. I did not want this feeling to end even though his cold body made me shiver; or maybe it was my nervousness. He slowly ran his hand down my body feeling my every curve. Bringing his hand back up, he landed in my hair holding on to it. Pulling my head back gently he left my mouth and trailed cool kisses down to my neck and back to my ear. The desire ached through me, and I brought his mouth back to mine once more. Finally, he broke our kiss and whispered in my ear, "I am going to have to leave now, but I will stay with you tonight. You will know I am here."

"I don't want you to go … please …" I knew it was futile to beg. He could not stay revealed to me much longer.

"*Trust. Me.* I do not want to leave you. Even though my manifested body is stronger than it used to be, I don't think my willpower is strong enough to stay." He grinned at me.

I knew exactly what he meant, and I shook my head in agreement. He lowered his face back to mine for one last kiss. When he finally broke our kiss, he spoke softly and shyly in my ear, as if he were afraid of rejection. "I love you, Alisa." He said and was gone before I could say a word.

Chapter 19

"Run Alisa, RUN!!" I heard Jaxon's voice calling out to me. I could hear his voice but could not see him. Everything was turning dark. I searched around me trying to get my bearings. I finally found the wall beside me and leaned against it to adjust my eyes to the dark. Suddenly I realized the walls were not solid … they were moving, and I could hear the sound of clicking behind me.

I wanted to run as Jaxon had instructed me, but fear kept me frozen, not knowing which way to go. "What is this?" I quickly pulled away from the wall. I shook my head focusing on my body, trying to find the ability to move. As I tried lifting my feet, I found I couldn't run. Something felt heavy, slowing me down. I hoped to hell it wasn't the sludge again, as I guessed I was in another dream.

Dream or no dream, everything felt real as the darkness expanded around me. I wanted to reach out and use the wall for guidance down this dark corridor but was too afraid. The walls had thickened as if a heavy carpet was on them, but I had to keep going. I had to get out of here! Where was Jaxon? My eyes were adjusting to the dark and I could almost make out what was ahead of me. I reached out to the wall again for support and shrieked when I realized the walls were not covered in thick carpet as I had suspected, but in humongous hairy black spiders!

"OH MY GOD!!" I shouted in panic as they began creeping out of the floor, ceiling and the walls. The sound of movement and clicking grew loudly as they began dropping onto me and crawling on my body. I could hear Jaxon running towards me calling my name, but he was still too far away to help me. Batting them off, I tried to lift my feet and run, but these hideous creatures were in mass! They swarmed me, falling all over me, in my hair, my face, swamping my feet, inching up my body. I screeched out in horror until my throat felt raw! Panicking, my hands were everywhere in a frenzy. "Get them off of me! GET THEM OFF OF ME!" I screamed.

"JAXON!" I shrieked out to him. I needed help! I was in a losing battle against these revolting creatures. Looking down at my feet, the spiders had won the war and were slowly binding my ankles with their webs. "HURRY!! They're all over me!" I screamed.

"I'm coming! I'll get you! I'm so sorry about this, Alisa." I heard Jaxon behind me. In the background, sounds of sadistic voices were mocking and laughing. Mimicking us with "I'm sorry ... stop ... don't." They jeered through the dark. "It" was coming, I could sense it. That thing I saw from the other night in my previous nightmare. I quickly turned my head to see that its black hulking form was charging towards Jaxon as he ran to save me.

Jaxon reached me first, quickly picking me up, carrying me as he ran. I was in a fierce battle with the spiders, swatting them off of me and pulling at the webs around my ankles. Jaxon, however, was determined to beat this thing that was chasing us. I saw the dark form following us as it pointed in our direction. The jeering, scornful voices in the darkness were deafening as they laughed and taunted. I was so scared, I put my head on Jaxon's shoulder. My fear made me shiver and Jaxon held me tighter trying to calm me.

"Where ... are you going? How ... how are we going to ... get away?" I stammered.

"Not to worry, Alisa, I will do anything to keep you safe. I promise, we are going to get you away from him."

"How? That thing is too fast!"

"I'm just as fast, you'll see," he said trying to console me.

"What is that thing?" I whispered.

When he spoke, there was fear behind his voice. "The Keeper of Souls. Some might call him ... Death."

"WHAT?!" My head shot up to meet Jaxon's eyes.

"Ssshh, keep your head down. The Keeper of Souls is sort of the ruler here in Purgatory. Now listen, I need you to be calm and not speak while I get you away from here. I swear, I'll get you out safely."

The Keeper of Souls was moving fast, floating closer, but Jaxon concentrated on getting us away from it.

"Close your eyes and whatever you do, DO NOT LOOK AT IT! Especially not in the eyes!" Jaxon commanded.

Shaking my head in agreement, I did what he asked. I closed my eyes and wrapped my arms tight around his neck, keeping my head locked against his collar bone. I could feel the coldness from the Keeper of Souls reaching us and swirling around.

In the distance I could hear the same deep dark sneering voice from my previous nightmare rumbling out to us. "You know the rules, Jaxon ... I have warned you ... she will have to stay and be mine."

"NO, SHE WON'T!" Jaxon shouted to the Keeper as he ran. In a whisper Jaxon spoke in my ear. "I need you to do one more thing Alisa ... Pull up a memory. A wonderful memory and study it. Think hard on it and don't let that memory go."

Of course, that would not be too difficult, I started thinking of this evening when Jaxon and I were kissing. The kisses of passion, the ones that led Jaxon to tell me he loved me. It was so beautiful a moment that I couldn't think of anything else. Jaxon grinned; he knew exactly what I was thinking. He could envision it too. We held onto that memory and felt the warmth from it as a glow surrounded us.

"I can leave you here Alisa; you will be safe. Keep that memory strong until you wake up. And please remember this ... I love you."

I opened my eyes just in time to see he was only able to mouth the last part when the darkness caught up with him, enveloping him, sucking him backwards into the folds. *Jaxon*!! I woke up with a sharp inhale! These dreams had become too real, and I needed to talk to Jaxon about them. I hoped he was okay! That thing caught up to him before I awoke. I wanted to believe he was fine, but I really needed assurance from him. God, I wanted to talk to him.

It was still very early in the morning. Too early for Elsie to be awake, so I got off Jaxon's bed, straightened it up and made sure the room was back to normal. I could not feel Jaxon's presence in the room and thought maybe he was downstairs or in the barn. I would check those places next.

No! He wasn't in either place. I had to believe he was all right. I mean, didn't he say he would always be here? Waiting for me? Maybe he was tired from staying manifested too long last night. I tried not to worry as I went back into the house to fix some coffee for myself and breakfast for Elsie. I hoped she was in a pancake mood because I was ravenous this morning and could probably eat an entire stack all by myself!

As I finished cooking the last pancake, I heard the shuffling of little feet coming down the stairs. With sleep still in her voice Elsie excitedly asked, "Did you cook all those for me?!"

"Not all of them. I have to eat too, you know!" I laughed at this cute little munchkin staring up at me with wide eyes. I may have cooked a few too many. Oh well, time to feast! When we finished up eating our last bites of pancake, I picked up the dishes and started cleaning up. "What do you want to do today, Elsie?"

"Can you take me back to that place in the woods where we played by the stream?"

Hearing her ask to be taken back to the place I found in the woods made me smile. "Absolutely! I liked that place too. In fact, I will pack us a picnic lunch to take with us."

Rubbing her tummy Elsie questioned me with her eyes and said, "I don't know if I can fit anything else in there!"

I laughed and shooed her on up the stairs. I was sure after walking all the way down to the stream, running and playing, she would easily work up an appetite ... eventually. I wanted to be prepared either way. There is nothing like a child whining from hunger.

We got everything together for our outing and stopped by the barn to make sure the horses had food and water. We could do some mucking out of the stalls later, unless Charles and Grace came home. I knew Charles would want to do it himself.

I was still trying to feel Jaxon's presence everywhere I went inside and outside. He was nowhere to be found! I was slightly worried, but it was still early, and I knew he had used a lot of energy last night. *Maybe he's sleeping in*, I chuckled to myself wondering if ghosts even slept.

Fun, fun, fun ... Elsie was such a joy! Watching her was super easy. We made up stories to go along with our "Hanley city" made of moss, sticks and stones. We played in the stream, and she proceeded to get me as wet as she possibly could. I was glad I had brought us the food and drinks. It wasn't too long before we polished everything off. I could tell she was beginning to run low on energy, so I suggested we start heading back. I just hoped we made it home before she got too tired to walk. I didn't want to end up carrying her and all the other stuff we had taken on our trip.

As we were nearing the house, I thought I saw someone near the barn. Dark hair ... Jaxon?! I didn't know if he would have been manifested so I could see him or maybe he was just practicing. He said he was doing a lot of that lately. We crossed the last field and walked towards the back of the house. I told Elsie to go on up to her room to 'rest', knowing that nap was now a dirty word.

Elsie took off. She knew she was exhausted and didn't fight me on the suggestion of resting. I decided to walk over to the barn to see if I could catch up to Jaxon. As I rounded the corner of the barn … Roger! My heart thumped in my chest. He gave me the willies, as the hair on my arms raised and my spine tingled. My "Spidey" senses were setting off alarms even though he had always been nice to me.

Facing my fear, I decided not to run. I was sure he wouldn't do anything stupid that would get him in trouble with Grace and Charles. "Hello Roger," I said casually not wanting to show any emotion towards him.

"Alisa! Hi! You're here … finally. I've been wanting to talk to you again." He said this as he looked at my face. I felt a little uncomfortable when he said, "Did you know, I think you are so pretty? I've been wanting to talk to you."

He said that twice now, "Um … that's nice Roger." He looked me up and down as if he was assessing a piece of meat before he bought it. I knew he was a little challenged, maybe he did not realize what he was doing. I wanted to stay neutral with my approach and not give him a reason to 'like' me. I was hoping I did not come across as mean. Who knew if he had a temper? I didn't want to give him any reason to hurt me, because that is how he was making me feel. The vibes I was getting from him were mixed. Part innocence, part malevolent. I wasn't sure where that left me standing here in the middle of it.

He took a step forward and reached out to touch my ponytail. I closed my eyes for a second to stand very still not wanting to encourage him.

"Your hair is so soft ... and I like the way it's wavy."

"Thank you," I said in monotone. If I had not been so tense, I may have found this endearing, but there was nothing endearing about this situation. I took a step back and told him that the Hanleys would be home any minute now and I had to go take care of Elsie. This caused him to frown at me.

"Why do you have to take care of Elsie *right now*?" He sneered. "I told you *I* wanted to talk to *you*."

I was frightened now. The horses must have felt my fear for they started snorting and pacing in their pens. Grey whinnied aloud and caused Roger to look. I took that moment to push Roger down and take off towards the house.

"ALISA!" He screamed at me furiously.

I ran as fast as I could towards the house, but somehow Roger was able to come up from behind. He reached out and caught my ponytail and wrenched me backwards. I screamed as I fell to the ground and Roger stood over me staring at me with pure outrage in his eyes.

"I told you I LIKED you ... I said you were PRETTY. You're supposed to be NICE to me," he yelled at me.

He grabbed my right arm and slammed his knee on it pinning it to the ground, putting all his weight on it. The pain burst in my arm from his kneecap. He stretched himself across my body to hold my other arm down. I wrenched my body towards him, bucking my hips and using my legs to make him lose his balance. I screamed "LEAVE ME ALONE!" at him, but this just seemed to infuriate him further. Just when I thought I had lost this battle with Roger, we heard a car driving up the driveway. "Thank you, God!" I said quietly. Roger took one last angry look at me, quickly got up and ran through the fields towards his house.

As the car came to a stop, both Grace and Charles jumped out of the car and ran towards me.

"Alisa! Are you okay? We saw Roger running off into the field." Grace exclaimed.

"Did he hurt you?" Charles asked as he was helping me to my feet.

"Not really, just my arm." I showed Charles and Grace my arm. The redness started near my bicep and ran to the crook of my arm.

"That is going to bruise; we need to get some ice on that quick." Grace said as she grabbed my arm and inspected it. "I am so glad we arrived when we did. I wouldn't have thought Roger could do something like this."

Charles spoke up then and surprised us both when he said, "He will not be allowed back on this property. Ever!" Then stormed off to the barn.

Grace and I looked at each other, we were momentarily stunned. Silently we walked into the house and Grace fixed me a bag of ice for my arm and told me to sit down. She was mothering me, making sure I was taken care of. I put the bag of ice on my arm which was a little painful to the touch now. I could bend it, so I knew it was not broken or anything as serious as that. However, I was going to have one hell of a bruise!

As soon as Grace was satisfied that I was going to be okay, she asked me to tell her the whole story. Steadily she was picking the grass out of my hair, as I was relaying the story. My body started shaking with the nerves from the fear that I had pent up during the altercation. Grace bent over and pulled me into a hug, suggesting we drink some hot tea. I had to laugh for a second. It was ninety plus degrees outside! "Couldn't we make it an iced tea instead?" I asked. She chuckled quietly and shook her head yes.

"Hey Grace, why would Charles say that Roger wouldn't *ever* be allowed back? Don't you think that's a little rash?"

"Well, think about it. If he attacked you, he could just as easily attack Elsie or me. We can no longer feel safe having him around."

"That's true, but doesn't Charles need Roger's help to work on the farm?"

"Don't you worry about that. I'm sure he can easily find somebody to hire on. In fact, with all the extra work we have around here, we've been considering hiring someone full time. Plus, Charles would never have Roger back now that we can't trust him around us or someone we love." Grace smiled at me when she said that last sentence.

She loved me and it made me feel special. I felt the same way for her and Elsie too. But more recently, I was even beginning to like Charles. I felt guilty about liking him since I knew Jaxon hated him so much. I was going to talk to Jaxon about how nice Charles was treating me recently, even though it *was* in a roundabout way. I personally think Charles didn't want anyone to see the softer side of him. If only I could find Jaxon. I really needed him right now.

Chapter 20

I let Charles drive me home. I was too afraid, exhausted, and stressed out to walk. I held a brave face as I was passing by Aunt Val and Uncle H.

"Wow, there she is," Aunt Valerie exclaimed.

"Feels like we haven't seen you for days!" Uncle Henry said jokingly.

"Yeah, I am tired. Didn't get much sleep last night."

Aunt Valerie looked at me and gave me a worried expression. She knew something was up, but I was in no mood to talk right now. I would have to let them know what happened with Roger sooner or later, but right now, I just wanted to get to my room. I said my goodnights and went on upstairs. Kicking off my shoes was all the energy I had as I crawled onto my bed and lay back against my pillows. I tried to close my eyes and rest, but the tears started seeping out, one by one. I put my hands up to cover my face and decided to let them come. God, what a terrifying day today had been, not to mention my horrific nightmare last night.

My nerves were shot, and I started sobbing. I heard the creaking of floorboards in the hallway and knew it was my aunt coming to check on me. She knocked on the door and asked if she could come in. It was her house! Of course, I said yes. When she opened the door, she was shocked to see I was crying.

Running over to me she pulled me into her arms allowing me to get it all out. When finally, I was down to a sniffle, she knew I'd be able to talk to her.

Pulling back so she could look at me, she asked, "Alisa, what's wrong? What happened Honey? Please, talk to me."

"Oh, Aunt Valerie, I'm sorry, I'm a mess!" Aunt Valerie gave me a moment to pull myself together before speaking. "This afternoon … I was on my way back to the house with Elsie. I had told her to run ahead and go lay down, because she was completely exhausted from our play time down at the stream. After she left, I saw someone near the barn, so I checked. And it was Roger who helps on the farm from time to time. He wanted to 'talk' to me," I said with air quotes. "What he was saying to me made me feel uncomfortable and I wanted to get away from him. So, I tried to run from him and …. He attacked me!" I proceeded to show her my arm and told her the rest of my story.

"Oh my God, Alisa! Do you want to call the police and press charges? I'm sure the Hanleys would support you if you decided to do that."

"No! I just want this whole thing over. Besides, Charles said he was not going to allow Roger to come back to the farm. Ever! Those were his exact words, and I'm sure he is going to talk to Roger's family about this to make sure he doesn't come back." I shivered as I said that. The mere fact that he only lived about a mile down the road made me uncomfortable.

"Alisa, this is not okay! I really think you should get the police involved," Aunt Val pleaded.

I heard the deep voice before the knock on the door ... "POLICE?!! What the hell happened?! What's going on?" Uncle Henry exclaimed as he walked through my bedroom door. I showed him my arm and we gave him the short version of what happened with Roger. "I am going to have a chat with that young man, and I don't mean with words!"

"No, Uncle Henry ... Charles is taking care of everything. He is going to talk to Roger's family, and not allow him back on his property. As for me, I'm done with this whole thing. No more talk of police, no more talk of Roger. And no more crying!" I said as I wiped away the last few tears from my eyes. I was tired and just needed to go to bed and get some sleep. I was exhausted and Aunt Valerie could tell.

"Let's leave her to rest right now, Henry, she needs her sleep. Is your arm, okay? Would you like another ice pack for it? I'll get you some aspirin for the pain too."

Aunt Valerie was gone before I could even say the words yes or no. Uncle Henry walked over and kissed me on the forehead. Taking my arm in his hand, he inspected the bruising. Shaking his head, looking as if it pained him as well, he let out a breath. "I am here for you, baby girl. You just let me know what you want me to do and consider it done. I still think we should contact the police, so if you change your mind, let me know." He squeezed my hand and started walking out the door, almost running into his wife rushing back to my room with the ice pack, aspirin and a glass of water. God, I loved these people!

That night I slept hard; no nightmares to keep me from my rest. I woke the next morning and could barely move my arm, it was so stiff. The bruising was really ugly now, deep purple and tinged with a yellowing color around it. *Great! Maybe I will wear something to match my arm,* I thought sarcastically. After getting cleaned up and dressed for the day, Aunt Valerie met me in the kitchen with a breakfast feast on the table. Uncle Henry was already sitting with a fork and knife in each hand trying to look like he was wasting away. I laughed at him in agreement, I was famished from missing dinner last night too.

We ate our breakfast, and they kept the conversation light. I told them I wanted to go back to the Hanleys today and Aunt Valerie looked at me inquisitively. "Why would you want to go back today? Don't you want to rest and give yourself time to heal physically as well as mentally?"

Uncle Henry shook his head in agreement. "I'm not sure that it's a good idea for you to go today," he chimed in.

"You guys, I'm okay! I promise! I really need to go and talk to Charles and Grace … I … I want to see if things were handled with Roger's family."

"You can do that with a phone call, you don't need to go over there." Uncle Henry said with a frown.

"You don't understand. I want to go over there. I'm not saying that I should go over there only to face my fears … I just feel like I *need* to go." I also felt I had to go and find Jaxon. I really needed him right now and still had not felt his presence or seen him anywhere since the nightmare.

With reluctance from both my aunt and uncle, they understood my argument and agreed that I could go. Aunt Valerie called Grace to make sure it was okay to let me come over. She readily said that it was fine, and off I went to see the Hanleys. As I walked down the long driveway, I kept looking all around to make sure I didn't see anybody. My anxiety was on high alert.

Grace must have told Elsie I was coming because I saw her bolt out the front door and run down to greet me. Giving me a giant hug, she looked up at me with a huge grin on her face. I rubbed the top of her head.

"What?! You missed me already? I was just here yesterday!"

"I woked up from my rest, and you were gone!" She said with a frown. I chuckled hearing her replacing the word nap for rest. But I should have known naps are for babies, according to Elsie.

"Well, your Mom and Dad came home, so it was time for me to leave."

"I heard Momma and Daddy talking about you. They were mad at someone and said you got hurt. Daddy is very, very angry about it. Can I see it?"

"See what?"

"Your hand."

"My hand? Don't you mean my arm?" I said as I lifted my arm and turned it towards her.

"Ooohh, that's ugly!" She wrinkled her nose up at me.

"I know, and it kind of hurts too!"

Elsie walked with me the rest of the way to the house keeping her hand in mine. I knew it was the only way she thought to provide me comfort and I loved her for that. Grace met us at the front door and let us in. "I tried to stop her from bugging you, but she couldn't wait to see you since she missed saying goodbye yesterday. Elsie, go on and play. Alisa will play with you later if she feels up to it."

"Yes Momma," Elsie said as she turned and skipped off while humming a tune to herself.

"How are you doing today? You, okay?" Grace looked at me with concern.

"I'm going to be fine. It's a little sensitive in the middle where I guess Roger's kneecap rammed into my arm."

"Oh Alisa, Charles and I feel so guilty. If we had been here, none of that would have happened."

"Grace, you two can't be here 24/7. It's going to be okay. I just wanted to know if Charles took care of things with Roger and his family." I shuddered a little when I said his name.

"That was taken care of last night! Charles does not wait to handle his business."

"W ... what did the family say?"

"Of course, they were upset and disappointed with Roger. But they completely understood where Charles was coming from and promised to keep him at home. They wanted to know if you were going to get the police involved. Charles did not know what to say other than you had not expressed a desire to do so. Are you going to press charges for assault?"

"No, I'm not. My aunt and uncle asked the same thing and were not too happy when I told them no as well."

"Are you sure about this?" She questioned me again.

"Yeah ... I kind of feel sorry for him, you know what I mean? And I don't think he really set out to hurt me. It's bad enough he can't come back here to work, I don't want to make things worse for him."

Shaking her head, Grace replied, "Alisa, you are too kindhearted for your own good."

"I know, that's what they tell me!" We both laughed as Grace got up to get me some iced tea. She didn't even have to ask anymore; she knew what I liked.

After we talked some more, I asked Grace if I could go see Grey before I played with Elsie. I told her that the horse calmed me. She understood and told me I could take one for a ride if I wished. I wasn't quite ready to do that by myself but thanked her anyway. I walked to the barn and saw the whole scene from yesterday replay in my mind. I closed my eyes and blew out a breath while shaking my head.

"Is that about me?"

My eyes flew open. I wanted to make sure he really was there standing in front of me. "Oh Jaxon, where have you been?!" I ran over and grabbed him, holding him tight.

Wrapping his arms around me he answered, "Purgatory." He grimaced when he spoke. "In fact, I shouldn't be here now, but I had to see you." He held me a bit longer, then stepped back to talk to me.

I fell silent for a moment, not wanting to waste the time to tell him about the whole Roger incident, but I didn't want to hide anything from him either. Besides, I really needed him right now.

Looking down, he noticed it. "Alisa! What happened to your arm?"

I quickly lifted my other hand up to cover the crux of my arm. He moved closer and I could feel the coolness of his touch as he pulled my hand away. He studied my arm, and a scowl came across his face.

Slowly and angrily, he said in a low voice, "What … the hell … happened?"

I winced and spoke softly, "I had an incident yesterday."

"That is not an incident. Talk to me, tell me what happened!" he demanded.

As my anger built, I could no longer hold my tongue. "What happened?! I'll tell you what happened! You were nowhere to be found when I needed you! When I had to fight off an attacker all by myself, when I was hurting, and I needed you there for comfort! And where were you when I needed you after that nightmare I had the other night?" I blurted everything out as the tears started to escape my eyes.

I had been trying to keep my temper in check, but I was wounded, and my emotions were still raw. I was angry and hurt that he had left me after my dream when I needed to see him, talk to him and couldn't find him. I was attacked and he didn't help me. Now *he* wanted to be angry over my injuries?!

I calmed myself slightly and looked him in the eyes, sending the arrow that would pierce his heart. "I'm sorry, but I was looking for you, trying to feel your presence. Yet, all I got was silence. I may have been physically hurt by Roger, but you … you hurt my heart."

Jaxon looked pained. I was sorry as soon as I had said the words. I took a step forward towards him and he stepped back away from me. I could tell he had to process what I had just said. With his head bowed and looking at the floor, he wanted to know more.

"I'm sorry, Alisa, please tell me what happened to you." He said in a strained voice.

I calmed down and told him the story of Rogers attack. "… your parents showed up just in time and he ran off."

I could almost see the steam blowing out of his ears. He was livid! Pacing back and forth I could tell he was trying to put the words together in his head before he spoke.

"Damn it, Alisa!! I should have been here to protect you. Here I was two days ago telling you I love you and the next day I fail you in the most basic form!" Jaxon finally stopped and turned towards me. Taking both of my hands into his, he looked me in the eyes with sadness. Shaking his head, he ran his fingers over my bruises making sure not to hurt me and continued. "I mean … I love you but I couldn't protect you or comfort you when you needed it."

"But why, Jaxon? Where did you go? Why couldn't I feel your presence?"

"The Keeper of Souls," was all he said.

"Jaxon, tell me."

"I'm sorry, Alisa, I have to go. I can't be the man you need me to be. Don't look for me and please don't … love me."

In a blink, he was gone. My heart was breaking. It was a crushing blow. I couldn't imagine my life without him in it now. He had made me fall in love with him, damn it! I could admit it now, I was in love with him. I had never felt this way about anyone and now in an instant, he was gone. I was devastated, I knew he would be tied to this place because of his mother's grief. So why not let me spend my time with him? Why would he not let me love him? The tears started to fall now, and I had to get away from here.

I ran away from the barn. Running down the driveway, I decided to run in the opposite direction of Roger's family farm. I took to the shoulder of the road and ran for at least three miles before turning to head back. The tears came and went as my running was clearing my mind, turning my hurt into anger and confusion over Jaxon. But the hurt in my heart would not go away. I wasn't sure it would ever go away.

Heading back to the house, I heard the car and knew exactly who it was. This was the last thing I needed right now, Grayson Henry Rutherford the Third.

Chapter 21

"Hello there, sweet thing," he said in a twang trying to sound country.

"Not interested, so please go away," I huffed.

Grinning back at me he said, "Honey, you're always interested."

Geez, how did I get so fortunate to catch Grayson's attention? I really didn't need this right now. My mind was still full of sorrow from Jaxon disappearing on me. I was standing there with my hands on my hips looking at Grayson when he spotted my arm.

"Good Lord, Alisa! What the hell happened to you?" he said in alarm.

I was slightly confused. This was the first time I had seen Grayson think of anyone besides himself. Was this real concern? Or was it just another show? I could never tell with him.

"If you must know, I was attacked by someone. But I thwarted him off. So, you best remember that in case you get any ideas."

"Alisa," he said in a calm voice. Turning off his car, he stepped out. "I would never attack you or try and hurt you. Sure, I love teasing you, but I'm not an animal!"

"Don't you think you should get your car off the road?" I said, trying to think of something else to talk about. This was a whole new version of Grayson that

I had not seen before. I didn't know how to react. It was easier when I could hate him. He always said something I could despise him for.

He gave me a sweet smile saying, "I think we are fine here. No cars around for miles. Now tell me about this attacker … is … is this all he did to you?"

I knew what he was asking, "Why? Does that taint my reputation for you?" I said sarcastically.

"Of course not!" He said with anger suddenly in his eyes. "But know this, I would kill whoever would do *that* to you."

"That is not necessary, Grayson, it didn't get *that* far. Besides, I wouldn't want you to go to jail for little ol' me!" I said putting my hand up to my chest for effect.

"Believe me, you would be worth it!" he said with a smirk.

"See … that right there is the reason I can't tell if you are being truthful with me or still being sarcastically flirty. Besides as you can see, I am able to take care of myself. I don't need any man's help!"

He took a step closer to me and took my arm into his hand and evaluated the bruises. He gently let it down and took my face into his hands carefully considering it. "No, I guess you don't need anyone's help, and I am not teasing right now. I'm terribly sorry someone hurt you and I want you to know I genuinely care. So, please let me know if I can help you in any way."

With that final statement, Grayson bent his head and brushed his lips gently to mine, letting go of me almost immediately. He stepped back into his car and started the engine. I was still in shock when he locked his eyes with mine and said, "Alisa, you need to see what is right in front of you." Then he put his car in gear and sped off.

What in the world was that?! Now I was more confused than ever. I did not need to add another thing on my plate. I was still dealing with Roger's attack fresh in my mind, falling in love with Jaxon, and then he leaves me. And now Grayson ... being kind and kissing me?! I had to talk to Nikki. She was the only one who knew about Jaxon and Grayson, and she was not going to believe this. But in the meantime, I had to face the all-knowing eyes of Aunt Valerie.

"Glad you are home, Sweetheart, maybe you can help me decide ... vanilla or chocolate?" Aunt Val asked holding up two cans of frosting.

"Seriously, you need to ask?! Always chocolate," I said grinning. "And what is with the canned frosting anyway? Don't you usually *make* your icing from scratch?"

"Had too much going on today. Besides, I am sure one can of frosting in your lifetime is not going to destroy my reputation with you."

We were laughing when she finally eyed me and said, "Did I see that Grayson fellow's car outside?"

I stopped laughing and rolled my eyes. "Really, Aunt Val? Do you not miss anything?"

"Not when it comes to the safety of my niece I don't."

"I was safe and anyway he is one of the most confusing people I know!"

"Why do you say that?" she asked as she began frosting the cake in front of her.

"Well, one day he is being all sarcastic and making snide remarks to me, and today he was super nice to me. I mean, actually nice, showing what seemed to be genuine concern for me when he saw my bruises. I just don't know what to make of him," I said throwing my hands up in the air.

"I know what to make of him," she said frowning. "He's a player, and you should not play right into his hands."

"Aunt Val, I know what you have told me about him. But he was truly angry when he found out I was attacked."

"Just be careful when it comes to him. I am not one for trust when it comes to Grayson. He is always getting into trouble, and you don't need to get involved with that nonsense."

"Oh, Aunt Valerie, you would think the worst of Santa Claus if he showed any interest in me."

We both laughed a good bit, then she said, "Just looking out for you, my dear. I cannot have you getting hurt again. And by the way, have you told your mother what happened yet?"

"Not yet, I was too afraid she would hop the next plane and be ready to kick some butt!"

"She has every right to feel that way … your uncle and I do. And besides, I think it will make you feel better letting it out. She is a good listener. Have some faith in your mom."

I lowered my head, knowing she was right. "I will tonight, I promise."

"Good girl, now go and work on your summer reading assignments until dinner time. Shouldn't be too long from now."

"Yes Ma'am," I said as I bowed and circled my right hand out towards her. "As you wish!"

"Oh, go on with you now!" Aunt Valerie said laughing and threw a dish towel at my head.

After dinner, I knew it was time to face the music. I called my mom, hoping she would not pick up. I kept repeating those words in my head … don't pick up, don't pick up, don't pick up.

"Hello my love! So glad you called me, I was missing you a lot today."

"I miss you too, Mom." I sighed.

"So, what is new today? Any new stories about Elsie or Grace? How about your summer reading … are you getting everything done?"

"Whoa, slow down Mom! You act like I don't call you all the time!"

"I know, it's just not being there is very hard for me."

"I wish you were here too." I knew I had to face the music and tell her. I had been putting it off, but Aunt Valerie was right. She would be very upset that I withheld the whole Roger incident, especially if I kept it from her any longer. "I am getting everything done. But I do have something to talk to you about."

"Uh Oh, is it a boy?"

"You could say that. Actually, there are two boys I need to tell you about. One is bad and the other I am confused over."

"Okay … tell me about the bad one first."

I proceeded to give her the whole story of Roger and the attack. She was not too happy when she heard it.

"Did you call the police?" She asked.

"No, Mom, I didn't want too."

"Alisa, you should press charges or at least get a restraining order against him!"

"Mom, it's not like that. He had a really bad accident when he was younger and is a little challenged now. I kind of feel sorry for him. I'm not even sure he understands what he did is wrong."

"That is not an excusable reason! Do I need to contact his family?"

"No, Grace's husband Charles took care of everything."

"But there is a chance he could come to you at Val and Henry's place! I don't like it; I think you should get a restraining order."

"Uncle Henry is well aware of what happened, and he is not going to leave us unprotected. Besides, Roger doesn't know where I live. Grace made sure of that. Everything is going to be okay; I promise."

"You should have told me about it the day it happened, Alisa. I don't understand why you would withhold this from me. Can you please explain that?"

I could hear the hurt in her voice and knew I had done the wrong thing by keeping it from her. Really there was no excuse good enough, but I would give her my reasoning. Hopefully, she would understand. "I guess I was afraid to tell you, because it might make you want to leave England and come home."

"Alisa, that is not a good excuse! Don't you realize that *you* are the most important thing in my life?! England is nothing compared to you. My *JOB* is nothing compared to you."

"Thanks Mom, I'm sure I knew that, and I guess I was simply scared to tell you. I'm sorry … will you forgive me?"

"Only if you tell me about the *other* confusing boy!" She laughed trying to put me in a lighter mood.

I could tell she was upset, but changing the subject was her way of letting it go and forgiving me.

She already knew about Grayson and how I felt about him and did not seem to be surprised when I told her about today's change of events. After she gave me a moment to state how I felt about what happened, she quickly added "I think he was after you the whole time. Maybe he really likes you."

"Then why be so rude and obnoxious to me?"

"Haven't you ever heard the old saying, thou dost protest too much? He overly projected his opposite feeling for you. He must have been attracted to you from the beginning."

"NOOOOO …" I wailed. I didn't want to even think of Grayson in that way.

Mom laughed at me saying "Now maybe the Lady dost protest too much!"

I rolled my eyes even though she couldn't see it. "Well, I haven't told you the end to my story from this afternoon. Grayson kissed me!"

"Oh, he did now, did he?"

"Not like that, Mom, it was sweet. Aunt Valerie doesn't want me anywhere near him though."

"Well, she should know … she knows everybody in town. If she doesn't like him, there is probably a good reason for it."

"She just says it's because he's a troublemaker."

"Well, it takes one to recognize one!" We both laughed, then mom told me "Just watch yourself and be careful."

"I will, Mom; I love you and be safe."

"Love you too and I need you to be safe!" We said our final goodbyes and hung up. She was right though; I did need to be more careful … with myself *and* my heart.

Later that night I talked with Nikki trying to make sense of everything that was going on. She was no help either, with the Jaxon nor the Grayson thing. She did rub it in that she had Grayson pegged. She began bragging how she knew Grayson liked me all along and that maybe I should go out with him, at least once. See if there was anything sincerely there between us. The problem was my heart truly belonged to Jaxon. As mad and hurt as I was with him, I did love him. Yet, like he said, we couldn't be together. It was not realistic! He was a ghost, and nothing could bring him back to me as a human.

"Are you even listening to me?" Nikki asked.

"I'm sorry, my mind is all over the place. Let me call you tomorrow when I am not so confused. Besides, it has been an awfully long and emotional day for me."

"Okay, call me tomorrow when you can."

"Will do!"

Chapter 22

Later that night I fell into a restless sleep, my dreams were all over the place. I dreamt of Jaxon. He was trying to find a way to apologize to me. I was upset and angry that he had broken my heart. I was hurting so much because of him and his decision to break up with me. A decision that he didn't even let me be a part of making! He looked dejected as I reiterated what he had told me earlier. He was right in saying that as much as we cared for each other, there was no moving forward. He looked at me with hope in his eyes, asking that I give him time to make things right. I did not know what that meant! He was an apparition after all, a human that did not even exist in my world.

Suddenly, Grayson walked into my dream and Jaxon was not happy.

"Hello, sugar," Grayson said as he kissed me on the cheek and put his arm around me.

"What the hell is this?" Jaxon asked as he looked at Grayson and then at me.

"What do you think, bro? I'm claiming my property," Grayson said eyeing Jaxon with determination in his eyes. "And why are you here, Jaxon? I doubt Alisa is into dating the walking dead."

"Uh, that's zombies Grayson, not ghosts." I could tell by Jaxon's face this was going to be intense. I turned and looked at Grayson saying, "First off ... I

... am ... nobody's property!" Then eyeing them both and staring them down I said, "Secondly ... nobody here is my boyfriend." Jaxon looked hurt, but I was only stating what he had already said earlier today. There was not going to be anything between us.

"Come on, babe," Grayson cooed at me. "Don't you want me to take you out? Go to dinner, or take in a movie? You know ... dating! It's not like the stiff over there can take you anywhere."

"That has never been that important to me, Grayson. And you would know that, if you could move your self-importance out of the way long enough to see who I really am."

Jaxon laughed and Grayson got angry and snarled, "What are you laughing at, dead boy? It's not like you even have a chance with Alisa!"

Jaxon's eyes grew dark and dangerous. Moving himself up to within an inch of Grayson's face, he replied in a low menacingly growl, "I can have you join me if you are not careful." Grayson took a step back but was undeterred.

"No threat is going to scare me off that easily. If it is a fight you want, let's go ... right now!"

"Stop it!! Both of you just stop!" I exclaimed, not wanting anything to happen between the two of them. Why was I becoming protective of Grayson? "This is ridiculous. Maybe I shouldn't talk to either of you!" I looked over at Grayson and smirked. "Grayson, I don't think Jaxon meant a fight ..."

"More like death!" Jaxon cut me off.

"That is enough!! I ... I can't do this." I held my hand up and walked away leaving both Jaxon and Grayson staring after me.

Jaxon shook his head sadly and disappeared as Grayson called out to me, "Alisa, wait!" I didn't stop. I kept walking away getting further and further as quickly as my feet would take me. Once I felt I was alone, I awoke in a cold sweat. This was getting crazy, my dreams, or should I say nightmares, were becoming regular and too realistic. I felt as if I had hurt Jaxon and it almost seemed as if Grayson were there, but I knew that was impossible.

It is a new day, and other than the crazy dream last night, I was feeling mentally better this morning. I guess talking with my mom and laying it all out helped me more than I wanted to admit. Dang if Aunt Valerie was right! I did have to talk to my mom about the attack.

It was such a beautiful day and not as hot as it had been recently. So, I decided today would be a good day to go and play with Elsie. I accepted the fact that Jaxon would not be there. I was going purely because I wanted to see the Hanleys.

I was walking up the long driveway and I felt the usual stirrings for the old house and all its magnificence. It was a beautiful house to behold, the rays of sun were shining down on it making it seem like it was glowing. I was falling into my usual daydream over the house when Elsie came bolting out the front door to greet me and snapped me back to reality.

"Alisa! Alisa!" She called out to me as she ran up to me, "I'm glad you came back!"

"Why would I not come back to see you, Elsie?"

"Momma said it might be hard on you to come over here, because of your arm and stuff." She said innocently. She didn't know everything that had happened.

I knew what she meant, though. Grace was worried I would harbor some bad memories about Roger attacking me here and may not want to come around because of it. I smiled at her saying, "No way, I would miss you too much!"

Elsie beamed at me giving me that beautiful face of hers. I could never turn that face down ... ever! "Guess what?!"

"I don't know. Why don't you tell me?"

"I got a puppy!" She grabbed me by the hand and dragged me off to a little doghouse next to the barn to see her new dog. Picking it up she held it up to me. "This is Puppy!"

"You named your dog Puppy?" I chuckled.

"I couldn't decide on a name, so I call him Puppy. And he answers to it! Look ... come here Puppy!" She called and the little dog jumped up and down on Elsie trying to lick her.

I could not stand it! Any more cuteness and I would drown in it. We laughed as the puppy licked and played with us. Grace came out to visit while I spent time with Elsie and her dog. She gave me that look that asked if I were okay. I nodded yes and gave her a thumbs up. Elsie was confused and shrugged it off because the puppy was *way* too important to worry over than me.

I asked Grace if I could go and visit with Grey for a while. "Of course, my dear. I'm afraid Elsie is too taken with her new puppy to pay much attention to you anyway." We both laughed as I agreed and felt no remorse leaving her.

Walking into the barn, I held no expectations other than to see the horse. I was a little sad that Jaxon was not going to be there, but it is what it is. I had to accept it. I went over to Grey and started petting and talking to him. He was doing the usual nuzzling. I was going to have to get brave enough one day and ride him. As I bent over to grab some fresh hay to feed him, I felt a soft breeze go by and I stiffened. I could feel the presence but knew that he should not be there.

I was unsure at the thought of seeing Jaxon. However, when I turned, I could not see him anywhere. I turned back around to talk to the horse again, when I heard a whispering in my ear. "Why in the hell was Grayson part of our time together last night?!"

Wait, what?! How ... who? I turned back around and still could not see Jaxon! I wondered if this was truly Jaxon speaking or was it something else trying to sound like Jaxon. But then how did it know about my dream? "Jaxon? Is that you?" I whispered.

The voice was stronger now and spoke mockingly to me, "Who else would it be, Alisa?"

I looked everywhere, but still Jaxon had not manifested. "I am not speaking to you until you show yourself ... prove that it is really you!"

Jaxon lowered his voice, "I cannot reveal myself right now, but I can tell you that I am quite unhappy you had a dream of me with another guy in it."

"How do I know you're not one of the Keeper of Souls minions, or the Keeper himself?" I started to get nervous now. Jaxon had said he could not come back to me and left because of the Keeper of Souls.

I heard him sigh, "Alisa, it is me, you're going to have to trust me."

"Give me a sign … something that only you and I know about." I felt a presence next to me and a cool touch on my forehead making an X with an O around it. I knew right then it was him. He should be the only one who knew what that meant. "You were there when Elsie told me the story!"

"Yes," was all he said, being curt.

"Oh, Jaxon, thank God it's really you! You had me scared for a moment. How come you can't show yourself to me?"

"Let's just say I am being watched, and I'm really not supposed to be talking to you right now. But I had to know … why was Grayson in our dream last night?"

"How did you know about the dream?" I asked.

"I was there! I come to you in the dreams where you meet me."

"How do I *meet* you in my dreams?" I was confused more than ever now. I thought I was just having nightmares, not actually meeting Jaxon there.

"Anytime you are thinking of me and seeing me in your dreams, I am really there. You are coming to me in Purgatory. Which is a very dangerous place for you to be." He frowned. "But you have not answered my question."

"I don't know why Grayson was there, Jaxon. That is all I can tell you. I saw him yesterday and he asked me about my arm, and we talked for a little while and … wait, Purgatory?!"

"And he kissed you." Jaxon ground out.

I was startled. "How did you know about that?!"

"Were you not going to tell me, Alisa? I followed you to the end of the property. Even though I had left you in the barn, I still wanted to make sure you were safe. I was determined not to fail you again and what did I see? You, flirting with another guy, and then you let him kiss you!"

"I was not flirting with anyone; he asked about my arm and was upset for me. It was not truly a kiss … just a graze over my lips. And what difference does it make? You made yourself perfectly clear yesterday that we were done. And what do you mean I meet you in Purgatory?"

Ignoring the question, he continued, "I was angry that I could not be here when you needed me, and I have a lot of eyes on me, constantly watching. I don't want anything to happen to you, so I thought it best we not see each other. So, tell me, what's the real reason you brought Grayson into our dream last night?"

"Well, for one thing … you *left* me; remember?! You said I shouldn't love you and then you disappeared!" I was getting heated now; his questioning was making me angry. "Secondly, Grayson was only being considerate of my feelings, it's reassuring to know that someone cares. Other than that, who knows why he kissed me. What difference does it make now anyway? As for the dream, how do I know? Maybe his thoughtfulness got into my psyche! At least he cares about my well-being!! What, are you jealous?!"

I heard the growl and felt the disappearance almost as sudden as it came. I didn't care though; he had made it perfectly clear that this was over. Without asking me might I add! He was also not answering all my questions either about Purgatory. I knew it was not fair to be so hard on Jaxon. Especially when he was dealing with this Keeper of Souls thing but damn it, I wanted to have some say in the matter when it came to us. I wanted him to talk it over with me, let me decide if I want to continue a relationship with him or not. After all, I loved him.

Chapter 23

I was stewing over the big fight we just had as I ran home. I spoke briefly to my aunt letting her know that I was going to work on my summer reading assignments in my room. But who was I kidding? I knew I could not even think about any assignments at the moment. I plopped onto my bed and went back over the words that Jaxon had said. He had talked of my dreams and how they were real when he was in them. Then ... Oh my God!!!

It suddenly hit me! If Jaxon was telling me that my dreams with him were real, then were all those attacks by the Keeper of Souls real too? I had to talk to Jaxon, he had to explain all of this to me. I stood up and started pacing back and forth. I wondered if I could conjure up a dream and have Jaxon come to me. Maybe I could talk to him that way. But would he even come to me? He was so angry when he left! I had to explain myself to him. He needed to understand where I was coming from about the breakup. And maybe in return, he could explain more about the Keeper of Souls and Purgatory to me.

Deciding to test my theory, I turned on a fan and laid down for a 'nap'. Closing my eyes, I forced myself to stop my thoughts from running all over and just relax. I was determined to keep my thoughts solely on Jaxon. I listened to the fan as it lulled me to sleep. As soon as sleep began the dream started and I found myself at the beautiful sunflower garden. The rays of sunlight were shining down on me, warming me through as I looked out over the sunflowers. The cast of gold glowed across the field as the sun washed over them. It was the most beautiful scene I had ever witnessed. I called out to Jaxon to see if he would come to me.

"Jaxon … are you here?" I waited, but no sound came to me. I walked further into the sunflowers wanting to feel their leaves and touching the stalks as I passed them. I tried again, "Jaxon" I said in a whispering voice. It dawned on me that I should not be calling out loud and letting the Keeper of Souls know that I was here.

"I am here, Alisa."

I knew he still loved me! Turning around, I saw him standing there. My heart swelled as I knew he would forgive me for our fight earlier. "Is this real now? Am I making this up or are you really here?"

"I am really here, Alisa; you are not making this up."

"I knew this would work!" I was so proud of myself for thinking of this. "Are we in Purgatory right now?"

"Yes" was all he said. Smiling at me he held out his hand so we could take a walk together. I could not stop looking at him. He was always a sight to behold. He took me to the back of the sunflower garden and picked a flower. I blushed when he handed it to me. Such a simple gesture, but the meaning was impactful. I knew he still had feelings for me.

"Why did you call for me?" he asked.

"I wanted to apologize for being angry with you earlier, but something you said struck me. You said our dreams together were real, is that correct?"

"Yes, just as I am here with you right now. You called for me, I came. Grayson was just an add-in, a part of your subconsciousness. You created his existence in your dream. So, are we going to be alone this time?"

I knew what he was asking … is Grayson going to be a part of this dream. "Not unless you keep bringing him up," I teased. "I am glad you showed up this time. I thought maybe you would never want to see me again after our fight."

"Not going to happen," he said, giving me that mischievous grin, displaying those dimples I couldn't get enough of.

I appreciated his quick acceptance that we were okay, even after fighting like we did. But now, I needed answers. "I think I figured you out, why I hadn't seen you in a couple of days. Then you showed up and did not manifest. You were protecting me from the Keeper of Souls, weren't you?"

He took a slow breath in and let it out preparing himself for our conversation. "Alisa, do you remember the nightmares you have already experienced?"

"Yes, I was going to talk to you about them. The one with the black sludge almost drowning me and the one with the nasty spiders."

"Yes, they were all warnings. You should not be spending time with me in this place. It is against the *rules* here in Purgatory. I'm not supposed to have physical, verbal or even emotional contact with the living."

"What about my first dream? Nothing really happened except the room getting thick in darkness and cold. I almost felt like I was going to be sucked into it. It scared me so much until you touched me, waking me up."

"Alisa, you looked so lovely laying there. I just saw you that day and had to touch your face." He chuckled trying to lighten my mood.

"Not funny! What happened after you left me the night of the spiders? Which I still can't get out of my mind," She sighed.

"Agreed!" Jaxon shook his head in agreement. "That night, when I told you to think of something special, The Keeper was chasing us, and I was able to leave you in the light of your memory. I was not so lucky; I was pulled back and well, let's just leave it at that. The penance for that sin I do not want you to hear." He shuddered as if the memory of it was more than he could bear.

I felt extremely guilty knowing that Jaxon suffered because of me when he wanted nothing more than to protect me! I could not love him more than I did right at this moment. "You saved my life, didn't you?"

"Yes, because I would never let you join me in this hellish place, Alisa. I can't let you die; I would never forgive myself if that happened."

"Stop talking about death. I hate what this place is doing to you. I feel so bad that you have to be like this!" I said, waiving my hand up and down to express I meant in his apparition form, wandering endlessly due to his mother's grief. "I wish I could get you out of here."

Jaxon sighed, "there is no way back from death, Alisa. But when I'm alone spending time with you … that is more than I could have ever wished for in this state I'm in. I feel alive when I am with you."

I looked down at the sunflower he had given me. It meant love to him; his father's love for his mother, and I knew it meant that he loved me too. I held the sunflower close to my heart and felt the love between us. He took my hand and brought me closer to him. I looked up at him and he took my chin and raised it gently. He bent down and captured my mouth with his. The coolness of his mouth was replaced with the warmth of our intensity of desire as it enveloped us.

Wrapping his arms around me, he held me, pulling me in tighter. He kissed me again, this time with more passion. Inflaming our hearts, the world around us melted away leaving just the two of us bound by our desire. He left my mouth and traveled his kisses to my ear where he sweetly whispered, "I love you, Alisa. Don't leave me."

I knew what he meant; he was talking about Grayson. He was worried about me falling in love with another guy, leaving him for the living. I turned his face so he could look me in the eye, I wanted to reassure him. "Jaxon, I love you." I immediately saw the relief in his eyes. "I'm not …."

I was cut off by the sounds beyond the sunflower fields. I recognized those sounds; they were the same voices I had heard in my previous nightmares, snarling and menacingly calling out to us. Our heads shot up and we looked at each other with fear in our eyes, we knew what this meant. We must have lost track of the time; I was supposed to leave before the Keeper came.

"Oh God! You have to get out of here, Alisa!" Jaxon said in a panic.

"How? I can't seem to …" My words were stopped by the feel of something moving in my hand. The stalk of the sunflower I was holding was shifting in my hand. Slowly It began to slither up my wrist as I tried to pull it off me. It wouldn't budge from my skin as it continued to wind its way around my arm. "What the hell is this?" I asked Jaxon in fear.

"You have to wake up or dream of something else!" He cried out to me.

Stopping just below my elbow, the flower stalk had twisted and wrapped around me as if it were a snake about to squeeze its prey. The sunflower stopped moving, to my relief, and I blew out the breath I had been holding. Hoping the worse was over, I couldn't have been more wrong.

Pain!! It almost brought me to my knees. It felt like sharp shards of glass were cutting into my skin. I saw the blood trickling down my arm as I watched metal spikes grow out of the flower stalk, digging deep into my skin. The leaves and petals of the flower were changing in front of my very eyes. I was holding a flower that had turned into sharp shiny razor blades.

I held it away from me trying to keep it as far away from my body as possible. Terrified, I sucked in a breath. I was too afraid to move! Fearing the blades of the flower would get too close and slice into me. The pain was burning from the torturous spikes as they grew deeper into my skin creating warmth from the steady flow of my blood.

The dark sounds of voices were laughing and taunting us as they were moving closer into the sunflower fields. The sun rays had faded, bringing in the darkness. Not because it was nighttime, but because The Keeper wanted the dark. "Jaxon!" I screamed out to him as the agony intensified. My blood was pooling around my feet, and I felt as if I could not take any more of this torment.

Looking up to him, I was begging for help, but he was beyond the ability to help me. He was too busy fighting the sunflowers that had surrounded him. They had wrapped themselves all around his arms and legs, pulling and binding him tightly. He looked at me with rage and fear, knowing he could not help me. "I'm sorry," he mouthed to me knowing there was nothing he could do to help me. The harder he fought the ties that bound him, the tighter they became.

The chaotic voices we had heard were slowly moving in through the rows of sunflowers gathering closer to us. They were bringing the darkness with them as the cold began rolling around us. A mist was gathering just beyond us, and I knew The Keeper would be here soon.

I could not help myself now, but I suddenly understood what Jaxon had to do. "STOP FIGHTING IT!!" I yelled at him. He looked at me like I was crazy and then he understood. Gathering his calm, it took everything in him, but he stopped fighting and stood still. The fight he had with the binds that held him, immediately stopped but did not release. He was a prisoner watching the war.

He looked at me with distress in his eyes. "Alisa, what can I do?!"

"What can you do?! This is all my fault ... I shouldn't have ..." My scream pierced the darkness as the sheer anguish of the flower stalk had twisted and tightened its grip on me; the pain was fierce. I continued to try and hold still as to not antagonize the flower to move my way or tighten any further on my arm, but it was pure torture. I kept my head down so Jaxon would not see the tears seeping out of the corners of my eyes.

"Oh please ... Stop ... What do I do?" Came the sinister cruel voices taunting with laughter. They were mocking us with merriment, enjoying the scene that was unfolding in front of them. They were too close, and the darkness was so thick I could feel it closing in on me. We were locked in this nightmare together and the torment was beyond anything I had ever experienced. I needed to see him, to know he was okay and have him assure I would be as well. I searched for his face in the darkness, but the darkness overruled me.

"Alisa, you know what to do!" he called out to me. "I cannot stand to hear you suffering, please do it!"

"But what about you, I can't leave you like this!"

"I will be okay, you'll see. What more can he do to me? Kill me? I'm already dead! But you need to go now! Try and think of your best memory."

"Jaxon, seriously? How? With all this pain?" I sucked in another breath, as I felt another squeeze. My vision was narrowing, and I thought I might pass out. I held onto my consciousness with all my might. If I collapsed, I would be hurt even further by those blades glistening in the dark at me, waiting for their turn to slice into my skin.

"I get it now, that is why he is doing this … so you can't think. If you hurt too much, then he thinks you cannot escape this. He has me bound to watch your torment, Alisa. He wants me to see you suffer … You have to do it now!"

I had to do whatever I could to get out of this place. I felt guilty leaving Jaxon, but my suffering was brutal. I did not think I could take much more of this. I had to block the pain and focus. I conjured up the memory of us right here in the sunflower field, right before The Keeper started this punishment. I thought of the love Jaxon had expressed to me and the kisses we had shared.

I concentrated harder on retaining that feeling of love, trying my best to ignore the constant anguish I felt in my arm. I saw the light … it was so dim, but I took everything I had within me to concentrate on it. I focused on that light, ignoring everything as it became brighter and began to move towards me. It finally grew enough to surround me. I took one last look at Jaxon beyond the light. He looked proudly at me for accomplishing this. I felt guilty as hell for leaving him there when I called out to him, "I love you," and walked into the light.

Seized from my nightmare, I woke up dripping in a cold sweat. The memory of that nightmare made me shudder; the pain was so intense. I looked down to where the spikes had been cutting into me, and oh God, oh God, oh God!! The trail of cuts from the spikes of the flower stalk were bleeding all over my sheets. I ran to the bathroom and turned the water on in the sink. Lifting my arm up in the mirror I could see the back side of my forearm where the cuts had led towards the elbow. The cuts from the spikes had made a perfect vining around my arm and into the palm of my hand. What am I going to do? How in the world was I going to explain this? My nightmare had transformed into reality.

Filling the sink full of water, I took a washcloth and ran it gently over my left arm cleaning all the blood off. The cuts were sensitive to the touch, and I had to get them to stop bleeding. After cleaning my arm, rubbing antibiotic ointment all over the cuts and bandaging them, I draped a towel over my arm so I could walk back to my bedroom. The thought occurred to me that I would have to look at my bed and see how badly I had bled on the sheets.

Checking my bed, I had to see if there was a mess. Sure enough, there was blood everywhere. At least it was not the same amount that had pooled at my feet in the nightmare while I was with Jaxon. What a relief that was or was it?! I couldn't answer that question because I did not know how I was going to hide these cuts. I was sure they would heal, but would they leave permanent scars? I hoped if I took good care of them, they wouldn't.

I put on a loose-fitting long sleeve cotton shirt and started pulling the sheets off of my bed so I could launder them. Looking at my bandages to make sure I ran them long ways on my wrist and hand. I figured running them that way would hide the beginning of my cuts that were visible. I checked to make sure my aunt was not anywhere around when I snuck into the laundry room. I took my sheets and threw them into the washer and turned to go back upstairs.

Aunt Val was standing there with questions in her eyes. "Why are you doing laundry right before dinner?" she asked me.

"I accidentally cut myself playing around and bled a little on my sheets. No big deal, but I didn't want them to stain." I hoped she was buying it, but I was desperately thinking about explaining what I could have done to cut myself.

"Are you all right? Did you get a bad cut? Do I need to take care of it for you?"

"Aunt Valerie! I'm seventeen, not two," I chuckled, hoping she would leave me be.

"You're right, I know … I just can't help myself. What in the world did you cut yourself with that would make you bleed so much?"

There it was - the Sonic Boom went off in my head. What did I cut myself with? I knew she was going to ask that question. Quickly I thought of my supplies for school. One of the tools I had brought with me was a drawing compass that had a sharp center point. We had used them in math class back home. So, I created a story around it to appease Aunt Valerie.

"Well, you need to be careful with those. They can be pretty sharp!"

"Tell me about it! It scraped me up good when I was flipping it around. I promise, I won't do that again!" I watched her face to see if she bought the lie. I felt relief when she said okay and walked away. I was not sure if I got away with it, but that was the story I was going to stick to for now. My biggest hope was that I healed fast.

Chapter 24

I decided to stay in my room the next day to focus on my assignments for school. It was the middle of July and usually I was finished with them by this time. Also, I was able to use that as an excuse to sequester myself and stay out of my aunt and uncle's vision. By dinner time, I wore the same shirt from the night before when Aunt Val gave me a look. I told her that it hadn't been dirty since I had only put it on the evening before when I felt a little chill in my room. I had at least worn a tank under it and kept it open like I would a sweater. She seemed to accept that and moved on to more supper topics.

On the third day, I knew I could not stay out of sight for ever. Aunt Valerie had asked me that morning if I wanted to go to town with her that day. I told her no, stating that I had a little more work to do to complete my assignments. Afterward I stated that I wanted to go see Elsie and Grace and play with the new puppy as my reward. She looked slightly disappointed but understood. At least I had not lied about the assignments being almost done. I had focused on them so much the past two days, trying to stay in my room, I was nearly finished.

It was noon when I finally finished my summer assignments, I decided to get cleaned up and go across the road. Before I dressed, I wanted to take my time and check out all my scars to see how far they had healed. I looked at my arm in the mirror and saw they were healing slowly and not even close to being invisible. I guess I was going to have to wear another long sleeve shirt today with band aids, my new style for the past three days.

I walked down the long driveway, wanting desperately to take off my long sleeve shirt. I was wearing a tank top underneath, but it was so hot. I knew I couldn't remove the top shirt, so I focused on trying not to sweat from the sun as it beat down. I did not even have the heart to look at the house as I usually did. I just kept my eyes on the dirt road.

When I reached the front door, I heard the puppy bark, and it brought a smile to my lips. However, I was still mentally down and gloomy. Grace met me at the door looking frazzled and seemed surprised to see me. Oh crap, I forgot to call ahead!

"I'm so sorry, Grace, I forgot to call. Is it a bad time?"

"Actually, it is perfect timing. I could really use you right now. I'm trying to prepare my sunflowers for drying and I have so many flowers to wrap. Would you be willing to help? I could pay you for your time."

"I would love to help you and you will absolutely NOT pay me!" Of course, the one thing that I did not want to look at right now were sunflowers, but I wanted to help Grace. I looked down at my arm and blocked the memory of the pain this flower inflicted on me and knew I had to move forward and let that nightmare go.

"It's so hot today. Do you want to take off your long sleeve shirt?" Grace asked as she lifted a large basket of cut sunflowers to the table. Sadly, I shook my head no and Grace took that to mean it was time to start. She gave me instructions for sizing the cheesecloth to cut and how to gently wrap the head of the sunflower. I tried to pay attention, but it was so hard doing so while in Jaxon's house.

"… and if you, do it right, you won't lose any of your seeds as they are drying. See, it's not too hard." She said as she showed me what to do. We sat there cutting out large squares of cheesecloth and gently tied them around the head of each flower. Well, I literally ended up just holding the stem of each flower upside down while she did all the work. I felt guilty, like I did not do as much as she needed me to.

"I'm sorry, I guess I don't quite have the touch you do. I'm not much help here."

"Actually, you are plenty of help. It is easier when the flower is held upside down than to lay them on the table and tie these up on your own." She paused for a moment and said, "Jaxon used to help me with these when he had the time. It became a special time that we had together, to just be alone and talk." I winced at the sound of Jaxon's name. I missed him so much right now and was worried about what could have happened to him after I left him in Purgatory the other night.

Grace smiled at her own memories and then continued. "Sometimes I can get Elsie to help me for about uh, three seconds before the whining starts. And Charles, forget it! He has too much work around the farm to help me. He figures this is my business, so I need to do all the work for it."

"Man, he's tough!" I said and she laughed. But I had a feeling he thought of it as women's work. Something that was beneath him, though Grace had not said so. We worked on the entire basket and took them to her drying shed. I handed them to her so she could hang each one upside down. When we were finished, she asked if I could stand to do another round. I told her sure and she left to cut more flowers.

As I waited, I walked around and ended up in the barn. I had to say hi to my favorite horse since I had not seen him for a while. Grey seemed just as happy to see me when I went over to pet him. I felt the presence before he even spoke. With my back still turned to him, I said, "Hello, Jaxon."

"Alisa, are you okay? I have been waiting around for you to come so I could check on you."

"Why didn't you just come to me in my dreams?"

"You seemed to have blocked me, but who could blame you after the last nightmare we had together."

I turned to look and see if he was actually present or just a voice. He was standing there giving me the charming Jaxon grin. God, if he only knew the effect he had on me when he smiled like that. I ran over to him, and he pulled me into his arms giving me a reassuring hug. Taking my face into his hands, he bent down to kiss me gently.

He stepped back to look me in the eyes. "Are you okay? You have not told me."

I shook my head no, and I could see the cloud of concern pool into his eyes.

"I have to show you something, Jaxon. I didn't think this would be possible, but the dreams are definitely too real." I looked around to make sure there was still no one around and slowly took off my long-sleeved shirt and removed the bandage I had wrapped around my arm. He immediately saw the cuts running around my arm like a vine from my palm to my elbow. I did not have to take off the two band aids. He already knew what the cuts would look like underneath. I heard a low rumble coming from deep within his chest. As he lifted my arm up to inspect it all the way around. His eyes turned to anger. He was beyond upset that I had been hurt again!

"How could I have let this happen to you!" He cried out as he started pacing back and forth. I realized this is what he did when he became angry, I had seen him do this same action before.

"Uh, mainly because you were a little tied up at the moment!" I said trying to lighten the mood.

He stopped in his tracks and looked at me. "I am not amused by your humor in this situation, Alisa. This is serious. You are truly injured, and all because of me and my selfishness. God! Why can't I just leave you alone? You don't need this!" He grabbed my wrist and held my arm up to look at it again.

"Jaxon, if you are going to get angry whenever I get hurt, you are going to have a miserable existence. I hurt myself all the time!"

"Alisa, stop! You don't understand. You would have never received these scars if you had not been put into that situation. I created that situation because I was breaking the rules ... again!"

"Jaxon, I know the rules too," I said trying to remain calm. "At least the rules you have told me about, and I believe I was the one who put us in that situation. But before the Keeper of Souls started his whole shebang, we had such a wonderful time in the sunflower fields. One that I will never forget." I stepped closer to him and took his face in my hands. "I still love you."

He pulled me tightly against him kissing me on the top of the head. "Put your shirt back on, I've got to go. Look for me, I'll be around." He disappeared and I rebandaged my arm up quickly and was putting my shirt back on when I heard my name being called. It was Grace. She was looking for me.

"Coming!" I called out giving Grey one final scratch behind his ear and ran out of the barn. Grace was standing by the back steps and laughed as she saw me running out of the barn.

"I can't keep you away from that horse, can I?" she said chuckling.

"Nope! You might have to let me adopt him."

"Or maybe you could get the nerve up and ride him one day."

"One day," I said with thoughts of Jaxon still rolling around in my mind, "maybe I will."

The rest of the day was exhaustive but good. Helping Grace kept my mind off my problems, plus I could feel Jaxon all around us in the kitchen. Every now and again I could feel the coolness of him behind me or touch the back of my neck. It felt wonderful since I was so hot wearing this damn long sleeve shirt. Grace had noticed the band aids on my hand and wrist and had asked about them. I gave her the same excuse I had given Aunt Valerie and she seemed to accept it easily enough, letting the subject drop.

Before I left for the day, I promised her I would come back in the morning to help her try and finish the rest of the sunflowers that needed to be dried. "Is 8:00 a.m. too late?" I asked.

"No, that is perfect timing. The family will be fed and off doing chores while you and I can get busy. Would you like me to save some breakfast for you?"

"You know me too well, Grace!" I said as I rubbed my stomach in circles. She laughed and called for Charles to drive me home. I tried to tell her that I was fine to walk, but she told me absolutely not. So, I gave in and let him drive me. He made small talk and thanked me for helping Grace with her sunflowers.

"No problem! I will be back tomorrow to help again."

"Should I pick you up? Make sure you are safe getting to our house? I don't want you walking anymore," he asked.

"No, I will have my aunt or uncle drop me off."

He turned his head and looked me dead in the eyes and said, "Make sure you do."

Chapter 25

I arrived at the Hanleys' house a little early since Uncle Henry dropped me off. I was wearing the usual "Uniform" of tank top and long-sleeved shirt with my shorts because the cuts were still extremely visible. I had a few minutes and went to the barn before going into the house. I could feel Jaxon as soon as I walked in.

"Wow, do you just stand here waiting for me to walk in? It's so early. Don't you sleep?" I knew it was a dumb question as soon as I spoke it.

"Uh, sleeping is for the dead!" He said and we both laughed. "Besides, I have nothing better to do today than wait for you. And why would I want to miss out on being with the most beautiful girl in the world?"

He made me blush, but I wanted to get serious for a moment and talk to him about Charles. I knew it was his sore spot, but it had been pressing on my mind since last night. "Jaxon, don't get angry with me, but I want to talk to you about Charles."

The instant scowl on his face told me everything. "Why would you want to ruin my time with you by bringing his name up?"

"I hate to say this, but I think you have to remove Charles as a suspect of your death."

"Why would you say that?! He hated me! Treated me like dirt, less even, like I wasn't even good enough for the soil he walked on. I also saw him running out of the barn after I had already fallen."

"Jaxon, I know he was hard on you and yes, he may have treated you poorly for which there is no excuse. But I have been around him a lot lately and he has even driven me home a couple of times. Was he friendly to me? No, but underneath all that hard exterior, he had a measure of protection for me. If he was pure evil, as you say, he would not try and keep me safe; would he?"

Jaxon fell silent and began pacing back and forth. I could tell he was processing this information and wrestled with the feelings he had for that man. As much as he despised Charles, he could not deny how thankful he was for Charles' protection over me. "I hear what you are saying and will think on it. In the meantime, you should go on into the house. I will be there with you today and I also want to watch my little sister for a while. She is killing me with that puppy of hers; so damned cute!"

"I know what you mean, she named him Puppy! I just love her."

Jaxon walked forward and lifted my chin to look me in the eyes, "And I love you." Kissing me deeply, he immediately let me go and disappeared. I touched my lips after he kissed me and felt its coolness linger. The passion of his kiss however burned into my skin. He had such an effect on me. My mind was racing, and my heart was thumping out of my chest. This must be what love feels like, I thought to myself as I walked to the house.

When Grace let me in, the smells of her wonderful cooking was wafting in the air as she led me to the kitchen. When I reached the table, I found a plate covered by a mountain of food. "Grace! Are we feeding an army? That cannot be all for me."

"I just wanted to make sure you had enough to eat. That is the least I can do for you since you won't let me pay you."

"Yeah, but if you stuff me to the gills, I will not be any good to you! I'm going to have to take a nap!" She laughed as I sat down and dove in. Grace could cook just as good as my Aunt Valerie, but I could never tell my aunt that. I tried to polish it all, but my stomach was stretching to its max. "Can I save the rest for later?"

"No need, the animals can enjoy it. I already have lunch planned."

"Grace! If you keep feeding me like this, I am going to be bigger than this house!"

"Oh, you know you love it!" She chuckled, poking my arm as she picked up my plate to clean up.

We worked tirelessly all morning, never stopping until she jumped up saying it was time to get lunch on the table. I lost count of the baskets of sunflowers we had filled, wrapped, and hung. I was of more help today now that I understood the process, and it helped to feel Jaxon's presence in the room. I could tell he was pleased I was helping his mother. At one point he rubbed my back and shoulders while Grace had left the room. I whispered a thank you when he finished.

"I am going to check on Elsie for a few minutes." He whispered in my ear.

"I'll be in the barn with Grey. Meet me there if you want to." I whispered back.

"Did you say something?" Grace asked as she walked back in the room.

"No, just talking to myself ... thinking I would like to go check on Grey if you don't mind."

"Not at all. You know, Alisa, you have really learned the process for prepping the sunflowers for drying. I'm so proud of you!"

I gave Grace a huge grin. "It just means I had a good teacher!"

"Get out of here," she blushed, "and take that break. You deserve it. I have to make lunch anyway."

It made me happy that she was proud of me, and I was in awe of how much I really did learn in two days. I walked to the barn hoping to see Jaxon. I wanted to tell him what Grace had said about me. I felt a presence right before I went in and smiled to myself. He made me so happy, and I knew he couldn't stay away from me, I laughed to myself.

When I went inside, much to my horror, there stood Roger. I wanted to scream but lost my voice in fear. I tried to stay calm, not knowing why he was here.

"I have been waiting for you, Alisa. I wanted to talk to you. Make you understand."

"U ... understand what?" I asked, my body began trembling in fear. Why was he wanting to talk to me? What could I do? He was not supposed to be here. I felt trapped! I knew if I ran, he would run after me and if I stayed here, who knew if he would attack me again. My only hope would be to keep him talking, hoping Charles or Grace would show up and help me.

"You made me very upset, Alisa."

"I'm sorry, how ... how did I upset you, Roger?"

"*You* got me kicked off this farm. *You* made me angry!" He said with an ugly scowl on his face moving a step closer.

"You attacked me, Roger. Did you think the Hanleys would be happy with you about that?" I said as calmly as I could. "Why did you attack me, Roger?" I had to know; I would have never expected him to be so aggressive. He had worked here for a couple of years and Grace had said he had never done anything like this before.

Looking at me with anger in his eyes, he hollered, "Grace is mad at me now. AND IT'S ALL YOUR FAULT!"

"How ... why is it my fault?" I stammered out.

"Everything was fine before you came along. I was happy! Then, you showed up and took Grace away from me."

This did not make sense! It wasn't like Grace was having an affair with him. I could not understand what he meant by taking Grace away from him. He sounded like a child pouting over a toy that was taken away. I wanted to know more, so I stayed silent and let him continue.

"Grace was so nice to me. She paid attention to me and treated me good. Then along came Alisa and now all she does is pay attention to you!" He said with seething resentment.

"Roger ... she's still very nice to you and talks to you all the time. I saw it."

"STOP TALKING, ALISA!! You do not UNDERSTAND!"

I clamped my mouth shut. The fear was so palatable I could taste it. My body started to shake, and I did not know what to do! Finally, he gained his composure and spoke again.

"I want Grace to like me again. To be nice to me and do things for me the way she used to. When I first started working here, she was kind and would talk to me; making me special treats. I liked that, but when Jaxon would show up, he'd ruin it. It was always all about him!" He took a deep breath and let it out, assessing me with his eyes as if trying to decide what to do with me.

Roger looked towards the door of the barn, making sure no one was coming. He continued. "I tried to make Grace be nice to me more. I wanted her to spend more time with *me*! But no, whenever I had time with her, Jaxon would show up and take over. It was MY TIME!" He yelled. "It made me *very angry,* Alisa. I had to take care of the problem. I knew that once Jaxon was gone, she would want to spend more time with me!"

Oh my God, was he saying what I think he was saying?! His desire to be mothered by Grace led him to murder Jaxon?! "What ... what about Elsie?"

"What about her? She's just a child, she needs her Momma like I do." He said it so matter of factly, as if he was just a young boy and not a young adult.

I should not say anything further, but I had to know. I looked at my feet for a moment, trying to get enough courage to ask the burning question in my mind. "Roger," I said quietly, "did you kill Jaxon?"

"You still do not understand me, do you?? *I had* to get him out of the way. I hid in the barn, just like I did for you! I knew he would be upstairs working with the hay that day, so that's where I hid. I knew it would be my chance to get rid of him once and for all. Then Grace would have to give all her attention to me! But now there is you ... someone else just getting in my way!!" Shaking his head, he suddenly looked back at me, "I have to get rid of you, Alisa."

I felt it before I could speak. Something solid slammed into the side of my head. I heard the crack and felt my face explode. As I was going down, I heard Jaxon's roar saying "NOOO!!" Roger screamed as Jaxon picked up a shovel and struck Roger with it twice, knocking him out cold.

Jaxon tried speaking to me "Alisa, can you hear me? You need help! Please, try and look at me, you are bleeding badly and need to get to the hospital. Please, open your eyes, baby. Come on try!" He picked me up and carried me as far as he could without chancing somebody seeing my body floating in the air. Laying me down gently, Jaxon ran up to the side of the house. He had to make his mother hear him and come outside, so he slammed against the door over and over. When he did not get a response, he knew what he had to do. Using every bit of energy he had, knowing it would make him disappear, he screamed out, "MOM".

I knew Grace would be standing at the stove cooking lunch. Would she be able to hear Jaxon as he tried to get her attention? As I lay there struggling to avoid the darkness of oblivion, I heard the banging of noise he made against the door and the shriek he made to call her. The door opened and I could hear her talking to herself, "That voice! No, it couldn't be!" She was outside knowing she had just heard Jaxon calling for her. She began frantically looking for Jaxon everywhere when she saw my body lying on the ground.

"Alisa!" She shrieked, "Oh darling, let me get help! CHARLES ... CHAAARRLES!!!" she screamed.

Charles heard her scream for him and ran to see what was wrong. Worried about Grace, he had not heard her sound like that since the day Jaxon died. "What is it? What's wrong?" I'm sure he saw me lying lifeless on the ground, blood everywhere. "Jesus! Call 911!" he yelled.

"I just did! I have to call her aunt and uncle too, but I can't leave her."

Charles reached down and put his fingers to my neck checking for a pulse. I was still alive, and he sounded grateful! "Grace, go get a towel. We need to stop this bleeding!"

Grace ran and got the towel, bringing the phone with her so she could call my aunt and uncle. Handing the towel to Charles she made the call, and in between her sobs, I heard her trying to tell them that I had been hurt.

"Valerie said they are on their way," she told Charles.

Charles was leaning over me, trying to keep me from unconsciousness. I could hear him, but he sounded like he was miles away. "Alisa, can you hear me? Wake up! Try to stay with us."

My eyes fluttered slightly as I tried to bring myself back. The pain was too great; all I could manage to spit out was "Roger, Jaxon."

Charles looked up at Grace, both were in shock. Grace finally spoke up, "Please, go check the barn!"

"Hold the towel to her head and gently apply the pressure. I'll be right back!" I heard him say.

Grace did what he had asked and was still crying as she knelt next to me when my aunt and uncle arrived.

Running to where my body lay on the ground, Aunt Valerie cried out as she sank down next to me. "Oh my God, Alisa!" Looking up at Grace she asked, "Did you find out what happened?" She took another long look at me and started sobbing. "Alisa, please … can you hear me?!" I felt myself fading quickly as I tried to respond, but no words would come out.

Grace spoke in between her tears, "Charles is checking the barn. She mentioned Roger briefly."

"Roger? Oh God no!" Aunt Valerie wailed.

Uncle Henry squatted down next to Aunt Val, trying to console her. I could hear the distress coming from his voice as he was trying to stay calm. He saw Charles coming out of the barn. "Find anything?" He called out.

Charles was shaking his head in utter confusion. "I … I am not sure I understand this?"

"What is it?" Uncle Henry asked.

"Roger is in the barn knocked out cold, beaten to a pulp! Henry, would you mind walking back with me? Maybe we can try to make sense of everything." Charles looked at his wife for a moment.

"What is it? What did you see?" Grace asked.

"I found the board Roger used on Alisa still in his hand. But I can't understand how he was knocked out cold by the shovel lying near by his body."

Grace looked at him and everybody locked eyes on her as she whispered. "Jaxon."

And then I was gone …

Made in the USA
Middletown, DE
03 November 2022